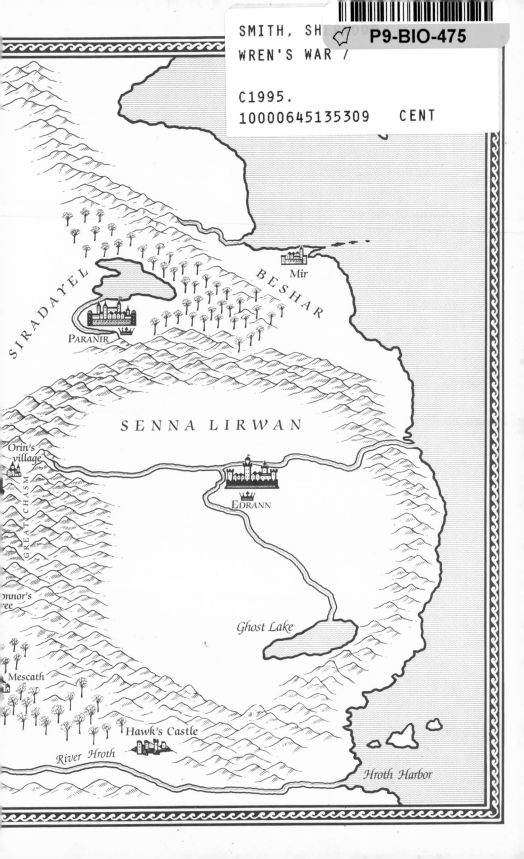

SIRADAYEL

BESHAR

Mir

PARANIR

SENNA LIRWAN

Orin's
village

GREAT CHASM

EDRANN

onnor's
ree

Ghost Lake

Mescath

Hawk's Castle

River Hroth

Hroth Harbor

Wren's War

Also by Sherwood Smith

WREN'S QUEST

WREN TO THE RESCUE

Wren's War

Sherwood Smith

Jane Yolen Books
Harcourt Brace & Company
San Diego   New York   London

Requests for permission to make copies of any part of the work should
be mailed to: Permissions Department, Harcourt Brace & Company,
6277 Sea Harbor Drive, Orlando, Florida 32887-6777.

Library of Congress Cataloging-in-Publication Data
Smith, Sherwood.
Wren's war/Sherwood Smith.—1st ed.
p. cm.
"Jane Yolen books"
Sequel to Wren's quest.
Summary: When wicked King Andreus declares war on the royal families
of Meldrith, Wren and her friends, Princess Teressa, Prince Connor,
and chief magic-maker Tyron, determine to defeat him.
ISBN 0-15-200977-9
[1. Fantasy.]   I. Title.
PZ7.S65933Ww   1995
[Fic]—dc20   94-36111

Endpaper map by Anita Karl and Jim Kemp
The text type was set in Sabon.
Designed by Camilla Filancia
Printed in the United States of America
B D F G E C

To my sister Lorie,
who, when we were small and things were scary,
liked me to sing
"Where Have All the Flowers Gone"

Wren's War

ROYAL FAMILIES OF MELDRITH AND SIRADAYEL

♔ : MELDRITH

♔ : SIRADAYEL

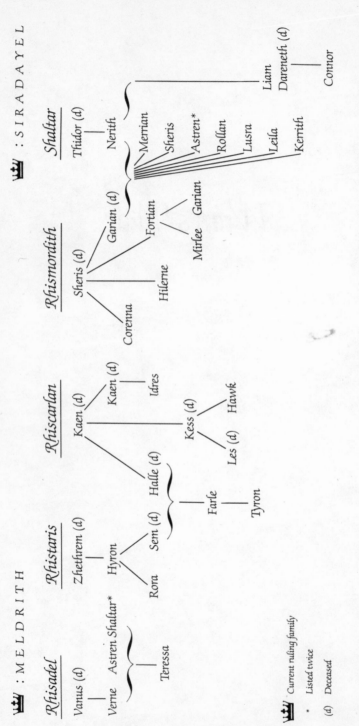

♔ Current ruling family

* Listed twice

(d) Deceased

NOTE: This family tree only shows connections relating directly to the main characters in this book. The four families are old and have intermarried many times. Anyone who wishes to know all the connections and all the cousins would do best to consult the Heraldry Guild in Cantirmoor.

Chapter One

*P*rincess Teressa looked past her horse's ears to the city gate. Cold rain stung her face, but she ignored it, hoping to see a short figure with thick braids sitting on a battlement and swinging her feet. All she saw were the customary sentries, alert at their posts despite the weather.

Wren must still be visiting her aunt up north in Allat Los.

Teressa tried not to feel disappointed. She'd known her best friend's visit was to last the month that the Cantirmoor School of Magic was closed down, but still she'd hoped that some kind of miracle would bring Wren back. During the last half a year, ever since Teressa had begun going out on diplomatic missions, she'd always returned to find Wren sitting atop the gate, waiting for her.

Not that I have anything good to tell you this time, Teressa thought wearily. She tried to straighten her aching back as she and her escort cantered their tired horses up the cobbled streets. She pushed her anonymous black cloak aside so that her gown was visible. Though she was muddy to the waist and her long braided hair dripped rain like a rat's tail, she was still the Princess, and she knew that eyes behind shutters and casements watched her.

It hurt to see how silent the streets were. The rare pedestrians hurried, glancing uneasily over their shoulders, as the gloom deepened toward night. A year ago—even last season—folk would have been coming out despite the weather, to

1

wave and cheer as she and her detachment of Scarlet Guard dashed by.

Not now. There had been too much trouble in her father's kingdom. *So we try to reassure people with our purposeful faces, so that they'll know Father Is Doing Something About It,* Teressa thought with bleak humor. *I just wish we really could do something.*

They clattered into the main courtyard, and stablehands ran out, torches hissing and streaming.

Two approached Teressa, a tall blond boy she recognized and a girl she didn't. The girl carried a golden cup in both hands.

"Welcome home, Your Highness," the boy said, bowing.

"Thanks . . . Alif, isn't it?" Teressa dismounted carefully. Pins and needles stabbed her legs.

She leaned against the horse. The girl stepped close, holding out her cup. "Something warm to drink?"

Teressa gladly accepted it. A spicy steam rose from the cup, and she drank deeply. A bitter undertaste made her tongue tingle, but she ignored it, glad of the cider's warmth.

"Ah," she said, starting to hand the cup back. Torchlight played over the beautiful shape. On its side Teressa saw the expected four stars, the symbol used by Meldrith's four royal families. But below the stars, instead of the Rhisadel crowned sun, there was an engraving of a bird in flight. Surprise made Teressa look up, but before she could ask about it, the girl took the cup from her hands.

"Thank you," Teressa said, then she glanced around for the crowd of servants who usually appeared when she arrived home. "Where's Fhleris? Or Tamny and the others?"

"Most of them are on errands. Duke Fortian's orders," Alif said. "He also said that you're to go to the Rose Room. Hot food is coming."

But I want to see my parents first. Teressa almost said it, but didn't. She never argued with servants; they were simply obeying orders. So she thanked Alif again, then shivered.

Though the cider had warmed her insides, her outside felt colder than before.

"We can go with you," Alif offered, moving to one side of her.

Teressa laughed. "After three years, I do know my way around the palace—"

They all stopped when a man's voice echoed from the torchlit main entrance across the courtyard. "Where is everyone? Where's the Steward? Find Helmburi!" Teressa instantly recognized her uncle Fortian Rhismordith, and from the sound of it, he was in a bad mood.

Alif and the girl exchanged looks, and Teressa said quickly, "You don't have to go with me if you've got other orders. But first, please take care of that poor horse. I can get to the Rose Room on my own."

The girl gave a quick nod to Alif, and both bowed and moved away.

Picking up her soggy skirts, Teressa hurried, not to the main entrance, but to a side door seldom used by any but servants.

Inside was warmth, and light. No one was about, though she heard someone's voice echo from the stairs above: "Hurry! Hurry!"

Teressa moved toward the door opening onto the main hallway, wondering if there were some kind of Court function going on. The Rose Room was not far, but she hesitated, then shook her head.

I'll go after I see Mother and Father, she decided. *They'll understand.* And at the prospect of seeing her parents, her spirits lifted a little, though her limbs felt heavy. *But before I climb all those stairs, I'll just rest a moment.*

She saw an unoccupied alcove and turned in to it, sinking down gratefully, wet clothes and all.

She had every reason to be tired. Although she had a splendid carriage, well appointed with every comfort, she and her honor guard had felt it safest to send the carriage one way, as a kind of decoy, while they rode cross-country on a faster route, Teressa swathed in a plain black cloak. The Scarlet Guards were the very best of Meldrith's warriors, and they rode fast and hard. It had been a matter of pride to Teressa to keep their pace—if they slowed it was not to be on her account. Today's ride had begun at dawn, with only two stops to change horses.

Teressa rested her forehead on her knees, trying to gather her vanishing strength. She thought of her parents, upstairs in the Royal Wing. As always, her mother would have hot chocolate ready for her, even if she'd had to order fresh three or four times. And later, she'd play her lute and sing all Teressa's favorite songs—the old folk songs that Teressa and Wren had sung at the orphanage where Teressa had been hidden for twelve years.

And her father would grab her in a bear hug and whisper, "I'm proud of my girl," even if her trip had not been completely successful.

Or a disaster, like this one was, she thought, wincing. She'd traveled through the northern provinces, listening to bitter complaints about how bad the roads were, how bold the brigands, and how trade was not being protected—yet how Duke Fortian had enough tax money to add a new wing to his palace.

My uncle has hurt the entire kingdom with the way he rules his province. I know Father is not supposed to interfere, but something must be done. If I'm alone with Mother and Father I can tell them everything I saw. She smiled a little. *And then we'll eat some supper, and maybe Tyron can come visit— or Connor will have gotten back from border duty.* Besides Wren, Tyron and Connor were her closest friends, one the heir to King's Magician Halfrid, and the other her royal uncle from Siradayel.

Thinking about Connor cheered her a bit. She knew it was wrong to favor anyone at Court, especially nowadays, but she liked him the best of all her relatives. However, she was careful to keep her feeling strictly to herself.

4

Suddenly her uncle Fortian's sharp, commanding voice echoed from the main hallway and pierced the fog of sleep closing around her: "The Princess—where is she?"

"We haven't seen her, Your Grace," a frightened servant answered. "Perhaps she went to the Magic School to see her friend?"

"Send someone over there," the Duke ordered.

Teressa got to her feet and moved as quickly as her aching legs could go. She knew it was cowardly—she should stand up and say *Here I am*—but she was too tired to face him just now.

Luckily, she knew just where to go to stay out of everyone's sight. On one of Wren's first visits to the palace, they'd explored all the rooms, from the ancient ones built six hundred years ago to the more modern ones. And then Wren had smacked her hands together. "Now we find the secret passageways," she'd said.

Her father had showed them their first one, but afterward it became a game: Every time Wren stayed at the palace, they had to find a new one. As a result, Teressa knew a secret way to get from just about any portion of the palace to another. A passage to the Royal Suite was just ahead.

She hurried into a narrow hallway, looking both ways to be sure she was alone. Then she pressed the carved berries in a wood panel. A small door silently swung out. Ducking in, she closed the door behind her, glad to find that the glow-globe that Wren had made still gave off blurry light.

"Mine only seem to last a few months," Wren had said in disgust. "When I think of the Iyon Daiyin making glow-globes that last centuries, I wonder if I'll ever be a good magician."

"Good enough for me," Teressa said softly now, touching the globe. "Oh, Wren, how I miss you." Gathering her heavy skirts in both hands, she started up the long, steep flight of stairs to the top of the passage.

It seemed to take forever. The last dozen steps were the hardest. She had to grit her teeth, forcing her trembling legs to move. When she reached the landing she blinked, but her

5

blurry vision would not clear. Sitting down abruptly on the top step, she leaned against the cold stone wall.

I'd better rest a moment, she thought, closing her eyes. She wished suddenly she'd eaten that hard bread that someone had offered her when they'd first stopped that morning. But she hadn't been hungry then.

It felt good to have her eyes shut. It also felt good not to have to move. Her arms and legs seemed suddenly as heavy as the chilly stone around her. Sighing, she sank back, and . . .

. . . jerked awake. A headache hammered at her head and her mouth was dry and bitter tasting. She started to rub her temple, stopping when her damp, clammy clothing sent cold chills through her. She felt worse now than she had right after that long ride.

She pulled her legs under her and rose to her knees. As her hand fumbled against the wall, one of her rings scraped the stone, the sound making her shudder.

"Come on, Tess," she said out loud. "Sooner you get up there, sooner you take these nasty clothes off and have something to eat."

She got to her feet, her head aching fiercely. Her necklace swung out and back, the heavy rubies banging against her collarbone. Fighting an urge to rip all her jewelry off and fling it away, she trod heavily to the next passage and started up the stairs.

As she did, her left hand fingered the deceptively simple stone on her right hand. She'd begun wearing jewelry only to keep attention away from the one ring she always wore—the summons ring that Tyron had fashioned for her. Not even her parents knew about it; the summons rings were part of a pact that the four friends—Wren, Tyron, Teressa, and Connor—had made last year, after the troubles besetting the kingdom had begun in earnest.

She finally reached the top step. The walls around her seemed to swim, and she had to pause and force the world to right itself.

Then she laid her hand on the door that led into the private sitting room. It was a place the King and Queen and Teressa retreated to when they wanted to be alone. On the other side the door was set into a wall painting. Would her parents be startled to see the painting open up and Teressa pop out? She sprang the catch, the door swung open—and she stepped into an empty room.

The lamps were flickering, as though someone had just moved out. Teressa sniffed. The delicious smell of chocolate wafted from the silver service on the main table, but Teressa could also smell her mother's scent.

"They must have gone out the door as I came in," Teressa whispered.

Then she heard noises out in the hallway. Shouts. And the scrape and ring of steel.

Forgetting her tiredness, aches, and hunger, she ran to the door.

Before her feet lay a groaning servingwoman, crimson splashed across her gray dress. And at the far end of the hallway were Teressa's parents, the King fighting with only a short knife against five or six sword-bearing warriors. Teressa recognized the warriors' gray livery though she had only seen it once before—when she had been a prisoner in Andreus's kingdom, Senna Lirwan.

Teressa took a step into the hallway, then the King gave a shout and fell under three slashing swords.

Teressa froze, her mouth open, but no sound came out. As she watched in horror, her mother backed protectively against the fallen King, snatched a lamp off a ledge, and slung it at the attackers. Streams of burning oil splashed over them, and they howled in rage.

But then her mother saw her and shouted, "Run, child!"

The foremost warrior whirled about and pointed a red-streaked sword at Teressa, just as the thunder of booted feet heralded new arrivals at the other end of the hall. Teressa gasped in relief when she saw the familiar long face of her father's Steward, Helmburi, at the head of a contingent of palace guards.

"Help us!" she shouted at him, ducking back inside the sitting room just long enough to grab a candlestick. Then she whirled around again, but before she could run to her mother, the Queen clutched her side and fell, giving a terrible choked cry.

"Noooo!" Teressa screamed, and threw the candlestick with all her strength at the man with the crimsoned sword standing over the Queen.

The next moment, Teressa was seized from behind. She had one last glimpse of the hallway, where flames licked at a tapestry. In their pitiless light she saw the still forms of her parents, her mother's arms flung over her husband.

Then the wet, heavy folds of her own cloak covered her head, and though she fought with all her might, she was borne off her feet and carried quickly in another direction.

Screaming into the stifling cloth, she tried her best to fight—without success.

Quite suddenly she was set on her feet. Clawing the cloak away from her head, she gazed in utter surprise at her captor. It was Steward Helmburi, and they were in the secret passage from which she had so recently emerged.

For a moment they stood there, both breathing heavily as they stared at each other in the steady glow of Wren's witch-light.

Teressa's throat ached. "Why did you grab me like that?"

"It's Andreus," Helmburi said, his voice rasping. "He has attacked Cantirmoor."

Teressa opened her mouth to insist on being taken back to her fallen parents—but no sound came out. Instead, the stone walls around her grayed into blackness.

Chapter Two

Tyron had just sunk into a troubled sleep when a cold hand seized his shoulder, pitching him out of his dreams—and out of his bed.

"Wha—?" he croaked, squinting up into the wavering light of a candle.

His roommate, Kial, stared back at him, eyes wide. "We're under attack!" Kial's hand shook, making the candle flare. "And Ferriam is dead!" His voice cracked on the last word.

Tyron scrambled up, yanking his tunic on over his head. "Falstan?"

"Missing." Kial was making an effort to speak plainly. "We're alone, and the prentices are in a panic."

They aren't the only ones, Tyron thought. "Where is everybody?"

"Laris is gathering them down in the library." Kial waved his candle like a torch, the licks of light dancing up the walls, making the shadows seem alive. "I'm just getting my books."

Tyron grabbed up his own bookbag and ran on ahead. Having been at the School half his life, he knew his way in the dark.

The stone floor was cold on his bare feet, but that was not what chilled him. Mistress Ferriam—dead? He thought of her round, cheerful face; the oldest magician, after Master Halfrid. She'd been teaching at the School before the King was born,

9

and always had charge of the School while Halfrid and Leila were away.

Light spilled from an open doorway at the end of the last hall. In the library Tyron found a knot of boys and girls—all the prentices who had nowhere to go while the School was closed—huddled together in a group. Anxious faces turned up toward him, all except that of a small girl in a corner who was crying softly into her hands.

Tyron looked at Laris. "What happened?"

"Attack on the palace," she said, her dark eyes enormous. "Falstan went to help."

"Ferriam?"

Laris winced. "Tona there was with her." She nodded toward the girl in the corner. "I guess she woke up with nightmares, and Ferriam was helping her—"

Tona looked up suddenly. "M-magic . . . uh-uh-attack," she stuttered between sobs. "Scruh . . . scry attack. I saw her. She—she was using her scry-stone, and—" Her words dissolved into tears as another girl moved to comfort her.

"Fire. Right through the stone," Laris said, her face anguished.

"Andreus," Tyron said in a hard voice.

"Has to be," Kial put in from behind. "Who else would know enough to strike through a scry-stone? Or be evil enough to do it?"

"And an attack on the palace?" Tyron tried to think. "All right, then we have only a short time—maybe no time—before they come here, looking for magicians. They aren't going to find any of you." His mind raced ahead. *What would Halfrid do?* "We've got to reach the senior magicians." He turned back to Laris. "You tried communication?"

"We tried. Won't work."

"Magic block. How about the Designation? No," he corrected himself. "If Andreus is here, the first thing he'll ruin is our transportation spell. We can't risk that now."

The three journeymages stared at one another while the younger magic students watched.

10

Noticing the circle of frightened faces, Kial said, "I think first we should get the prenties to safety."

"Then we've got to figure out a way to get past the ward-spells and summon Halfrid and Leila," Laris added.

"And we've got to help the King and Queen," Tyron put in.

"That's your job," Laris said soberly.

Kial nodded. "You're the best at the kind of magic that will take."

"And I'm the best among us at scrying," Laris said briskly. "So I'll work on the communication." No one mentioned Mistress Ferriam's terrible end, but Tyron knew that they were all thinking of it.

"No one seems to need a journeymage healer," Kial said—making a valiant effort, Tyron thought, at sounding cheerful. "So perhaps I ought to find us a bolt-hole. Do you think we should risk running for the Free Vale or try to hole up somewhere closer?"

Tyron shook his head. "If it really is Andreus, he'll be rooting out magicians first chance he can get, which means anywhere we go we are a danger to the people who hide us. The Free Vale is a Haven—it was originally made for hiding magicians. If we get separated we can meet there and plan what to do next."

If we're still alone. No one said that out loud either. But he could tell they were all thinking it, even Tona, who had gotten control of her weeping and sat, silent and red-eyed, listening.

Kial looked up, his face full of sudden hope. "If we go to the Haven, maybe those strange old sorcerer twins will help us."

"But they aren't there," Tyron said. "Disappeared for good a year ago. Halfrid told me not long before he left that they are in the east, chasing whoever it was who trained Andreus. It looks like we are on our own." Tyron felt his throat tighten unexpectedly. He knew he should say something more—something heartening—but the words would not come.

For a long moment the little group looked at one another.

11

It was Kial who broke the silence, heaving a sigh so deep it made his shoulders go up and down. "Come on, you prenties, we've got our orders. Let's stop in at the kitchen and raid it for stores, then we'll go to the stable and grab all our horses so the Lirwanis can't get them, shall we?" And as they jumped up, he went on in a cheery voice, "Come now, no panic. We're faster if we're orderly. Shall we repeat together the Crisis Rules?"

And several young, high voices quavered obediently, " 'A calm and clear mind hears what must be heard . . .' "

Tyron and Laris waited while they all filed out, then Laris said, "Do we even have any defense spells?"

"I don't know," Tyron said. "We've heard all our lives that working for peace and harmony are the only proper goals for magicians, so I won't find much in the newer books. Perhaps the old records . . ."

He broke off when they heard a distant crash. Tyron sprang to a window, saw the orange flare of fire at the School's front entrance.

"They're already here. I hope Kial gets the prenties out fast."

"Let's bind the library," Laris said, her voice taut.

Tyron nodded, and together they raced to the other end of the hall. The huge building was very old, and like in most old buildings in Cantirmoor, rooms and halls and stairways had been added over the centuries in varying styles. Newcomers had to learn to navigate.

In the face of mounting troubles, Master Halfrid had worried about the central library, which was where the magicians kept all the spells and enchantments discovered by the masters and students over the years. Halfrid had known that it was unlikely he could make an enchantment powerful enough to ward against a determined villain such as Andreus, who thought nothing of destroying anything in his path. Instead he had concocted a simple ward based on an illusion, but one that would be difficult to detect and break because of its very simplicity. Using the confusing building to advantage, the spell made the doors in the area of the library seem to lead the wrong way.

Running through the central part of the building, Tyron and Laris cast the spell repeatedly. When they reached the ground floor, they heard shouts and crashes at the other end. Looking at each other in the leaping light of the fires outside, they paused for breath.

"Kial should be well away by now," Laris said, leaning on a windowsill and clutching her magic bag tightly against her. "We'd better get out ourselves." She threw the window wide open.

Tyron looked outside, then turned back to Laris. "Go ahead," he said. "I think I'll stay here a bit."

"But they're burning the place down," she protested.

"No. Andreus will want to snoop out our spells first. They're trying to flush anyone still inside. But—" Again Tyron's throat tightened at the thought of the iron tread of Senna Lirwani soldiers tramping through the beloved halls, kicking and smashing things just to be destructive. He said fiercely, "But why let them have it easy? I'm going to stay and spellcast some of Wren's booby traps."

"Wren." Laris gave an unsteady laugh. "I wish she were here. But I'll stay and help, if you'll tell me what to do."

So they dashed toward the Masters' chambers, and Tyron yanked his book out of his bag and flipped through it.

Wren's magic was not strong yet, and her spells had a tendency to backfire, but she had a knack for using perfectly ordinary objects in imaginative ways.

As a joke, just before she'd left to visit her aunt, Wren had concocted a spell to make a pair of shoes rise from a closet floor and kick their owner. Tyron and Laris now converted her spell so that the shoes in all the dormitory rooms would fling themselves at the invaders as soon as they entered. Then Tyron altered the spell so that the heavy furniture in the refectory would hurl itself at entering soldiery.

When they reached the studies, they used their stronger

magic again, so when the doors were opened, the draft would send all the small objects in the room whirling toward the luckless person who entered.

In the kitchen, they got plates and pans to stick to the ceiling, ready to drop on unsuspecting entrants. And everywhere they cast illusions: holes to yawn in the floors, monsters to pop out of cupboards, and shadows to flicker and move in the corners of rooms.

Tyron and Laris laughed with abandon after each trick was completed, sometimes slapping each other in an excess of emotion that Tyron felt could turn suddenly to tears. Laris and he had never been particularly close. She was a solid student, her focus on the communication skills that were his weakest area—and the furthest from his interests. But now they behaved like the best of friends as they ran through their home, making it as unwelcome as possible for the invaders.

Working rapidly, Tyron watched their successes register in Laris's long, flushed face and shining black eyes, but secretly he wished his true best friends were there. Wren with her wit and imagination, Connor with his insight and sword skills—and beautiful, bright Teressa, the future Queen.

"One more," Laris gasped, leaning against a wall.

"One more," he agreed, bringing mind and heart back to the present.

They left only when they heard sudden shouts of rage echoing down a hall. The unwelcome visitors had found their first booby trap.

Snickering helplessly, Tyron and Laris climbed out into the shrubbery and ran through the garden, where only days ago they had lain in the grass, studying and talking and staring up at the peaceful autumn sky.

When they reached the low hills beyond the School, both looked back. By now fires gleamed in several windows on the ground floor, and the faint sounds of shouts and smashing glass reached them.

Tyron's laughter disappeared, and he felt grief and anger

taking its place. Laris was silent, the glow of the fires flickering in her dark eyes.

"We'd better go," Tyron said. He wished again that Connor and Wren were with him. *I wish I knew if Teressa were safe.*

Tears sparkled as they dropped down the front of Laris's journeymage tunic. She dashed her wrist across her eyes. "I'm going to find a safe place and try my scry-stone until I contact someone to help us."

"I will check on the palace," Tyron said. "Try to find Falstan."

Laris touched his shoulder and then turned away, her mass of long black hair helping her blend into the nightscape.

Tyron started walking north, his pace gradually increasing.

When his summons ring flashed, he was already running his hardest.

Chapter Three

$\mathcal{T}$eressa woke to find herself gripped in someone's arms, her head jouncing against a shoulder in the rhythm of a galloping horse. She could not see—a fold of her wet cloak was still wrapped over her head. Memory of the fighting flooded back, and with it the terrifying thought: *Helmburi captured me. Has he betrayed us?*

She had to get away, to find—

Her mind veered away from the memory of the two figures lying so still near the burning tapestry, and she shuddered. "Don't move, Highness," came Helmburi's voice. "We are on a cliff edge, and we might overbalance."

A cliff edge? She gritted her teeth, keeping her body stiff and still. Her mind raced along, faster than the horse, making plans for her escape.

It did not seem long after that the horse slowed, then stopped. Helmburi dismounted first, then pulled her off the horse and carried her a short distance. At last she was set gently on her feet, and the cloak was even more gently unwrapped from over her head. Teressa caught a glimpse of a bare cottage room lit by the cold blue light of glow-globes above an empty fireplace.

Before she could speak, Helmburi dropped on one knee before her and pressed a long knife into her numb fingers. His head bowed, his neck bare, he said: "Strike if you must, Highness, for my disobedience to your wishes, and for prisoning you against your will. May I give my reasons?"

Teressa stared down at the gooseflesh on the man's neck and felt a weird kind of laugh bubble in her throat. Recognizing the threat of hysteria, she bit it back and flung down the knife. "Speak," she said. "I'm glad you had a reason—and I think I've seen enough blood for one night."

Still kneeling, Helmburi lifted his head. Teressa looked at the exhausted, homely face, the grief-stricken eyes. Helmburi had been her father's Steward since both were teens. *Same age as I am now,* she thought.

"It was Duke Fortian's orders," he said. "If the King and Queen were to fall, I was to find you and take you promptly to a safe place. He said you'd try to fight, to argue, and I was to bring you, and you'd see reason later. You can't sacrifice yourself," he added, his voice quavering on the last word. "The kingdom will rally to your name. They need you."

Teressa sank into a chair, then leaned forward and pulled at Helmburi's shoulder. "Please. Sit down, Helmburi. You have to be as tired as I am," she said. "Tell me what has happened."

He rose, then sat on a bench, his posture stiff, as though he were uncomfortable about the breach of etiquette but too worn out to do otherwise.

"Just after you arrived, there was an attack by brigands at the west end of the city," he said. "It turned out to be a subterfuge, soldiers of Senna Lirwan disguised, fighting just to draw off the palace guard. We were evacuating people in the palace, but the King and Queen insisted on staying until you were found." He blinked. "Where were you, Princess Teressa? You arrived at sunset, and it is long past midnight."

"In the passage," Teressa said, surprised. "I—I took a nap." A thought hit her then, like a blow. "That cider I drank—it must have had a sleep elixir in it." She knuckled her stinging eyes. "So . . . my parents . . . would have been safely away . . . if I hadn't fallen asleep?"

Helmburi shook his head quickly. "The King and Queen would not risk being parted from you again, though Duke Fortian counseled just that. But in truth, we thought the palace safe enough."

17

Teressa bit her lip, fiercely willing herself to think, to stay in control. "Magic safeguards. Palace was protected—wasn't it?"

"Against magic attack," Helmburi said. "But there was no magic involved in this." He looked perplexed. "One of the reasons why Master Halfrid and Mistress Leila closed the School and went off, because they know so little about the magic of warfare." Helmburi let out a long sigh. "The principal magicians away and the greater part of the Scarlet Guard at the border, fighting brigands. This was very carefully worked out."

Teressa closed her hands together tightly. "How can we find out what is happening now?"

"I will return to the city and try to find the Duke. I know two rallying places he might be," Helmburi said. "You shall be safe enough here," he added. "I will build you a fire first, and there is some food in the cupboard—dried fruit and some journeycakes."

Teressa nodded. "Do that," she said. "Bring me news, so I'll know what to do to help." She tried to sound firm, but her voice was hoarse.

Helmburi bowed low and then turned to set up a fire. When the flames were roaring brightly, he promised he would return as soon as he could, and he went into the tiny stable adjacent, where his horse waited, still wet from the earlier journey.

Teressa listened to him ride away, then discovered that she was shaking. She moved close to the fire and held out her hands to the bright flames.

"I'm going to be practical," she said. "I'm going to plan, just as soon as I know something—" Her eyes caught on the glitter of one of her ring stones, and she remembered her summons ring.

Snatching it off, she held it in both hands and closed her eyes, muttering the magic phrase that Wren and Tyron had rehearsed so many times with her. "With magic, you have to be exact," Wren had said, though the magical words did not seem to make any sense.

"... *Khiza chorean Tyron; Khiza chorean Connor; Khiza chorean Wren,*" she finished, then she pushed the ring back onto her finger and scooted closer to the fire. Her wet gown seemed icy now, and she couldn't seem to stop shivering.

I've got to get warm, she thought. *That has to be my first job. I cannot help if I am sick.* But as she stared at the fire, she saw again the flames licking at the tapestry, and next to it—

"I'm in charge now. I have to be practical," she said out loud.

She had to be practical because she was now alone. But she couldn't close out the memories.

Three years were all we had. And now my parents are gone.

Her father's honest gaze, her mother's sweet voice. Gone.

The fire blurred. She dropped her head onto her arms, and wept.

Chapter Four

*I*s that Andreus?"

Prince Connor Shaltar, youngest son of the Queen of Siradayel, blinked against the orange glare of the distant torches.
All he could see were silhouettes of restless warriors—some on
horseback, most on foot.

Marit Limmeran, heir to the Baron Tamsal, nudged Connor. "You know what he looks like, don't you?"

"I saw him," Connor said. "Three years ago." He blinked,
trying to rid his eyes of the road grit that made the torches
brandished by the distant Lirwanis seem ringed. The patrol
he'd recently been assigned to had been riding since dawn, after
a week at the border.

All they'd thought of was getting home. Using back roads
to cut short their journey, they had crested a hill above Cantirmoor, to be met with the shocking sight of the city in flames.

Mistress Thule, their patrol leader, had said only, "We'll
fall back to Lookout Hill. I'll spy ahead—I'm fastest alone."

They'd ridden higher, to the place where the east road
crossed the north. She ordered Connor and Marit to dismount
and hide on the promontory above the crossroads while the
rest of the patrol removed with the horses to a short distance
up the hill. "I'll be back soon's I can," she'd said. "You wait
here. Don't peer over the rocks, peer around—through those
bushes. Remember what to look for?"

Connor and Marit both nodded. " 'Count them,' " Connor repeated. " 'Note what arms they carry, what uniform they

wear, formation they move in, supplies they carry; if they have special gear or a magician along.' "

The tough old campaigner had departed, and Marit and Connor had belly-crawled into position, then waited. Nothing had happened for a long time—nothing but a short, fierce rain squall. Then one patrol of Lirwanis rode into view, and instead of passing by, they milled around, waiting. The next group came shortly thereafter, riding up the other road.

"*Hsst,* Connor. That big one on the bay—that him?"

"No," Connor said. "He's short and skinny."

Marit sighed. "What are they waiting for?"

"Sh! Someone's talking. Maybe we'll hear some words."

"Sure—in Lirwani."

"I know some," came the quiet, laconic voice of Mistress Thule.

"She's finally back," Marit whispered into Connor's ear. "Now we'll find out what's going on." In the light of the Lirwanis' torches Connor saw him grinning with excitement.

"Quiet, let me listen," Mistress Thule cautioned, elbowing up next to them. Connor squinted down from between two boulders, watching the mass of soldiery. The two groups were obviously waiting for someone. Andreus?

A shift in the milling soldiers made Connor's heart thump. The mass suddenly separated into two groups, and down the center rode a tight formation of shield-bearing warriors. These parted and there, limned in torchlight, was a slim male figure on horseback. It was too far away, and too dark, to see features, but Connor caught the gleam of long blond hair—and then the figure slung his cloak carelessly back, a gesture of arrogant grace, and suddenly Connor knew.

"That's Andreus."

No one breathed as they listened, but all they heard was the rise and fall of a single voice. Even at this distance the sarcastic edge of that voice carried. Connor clenched his fists, wishing he were high enough in the hills to have access to his own peculiar magic. Then he could . . . he could . . .

Fool, he told himself. *What can you do except dump a bad*

21

storm on them, which will accomplish nothing besides leading Andreus to you? For his magic was an odd weather magic, and he had access to it only when he was in the mountains.

A final, languid gesture of command from Andreus, and his followers gave a great shout. At once the mass split into four smaller patrols and rode out in all four directions.

"You've seen him," Mistress Thule said quietly. "Now back up. Slowly."

They did, no one speaking until they were on the narrow trail leading straight up the mountain.

Mistress Thule brought them to a halt under a thick tree. Connor could barely see shapes in the dark, but his ears caught every crunch of boots on rock, and the short, rasping breathing of the others.

"All right," she said. "Here's the word. Lirwanis have taken Cantirmoor. Not easily, though. Heavy fighting, especially south end of the city."

Connor immediately thought of Teressa. "Where's the King?"

"No real news yet," Mistress Thule said. "Listen. We've had evacuation plans in place. Scarlet Guard will be helping with that. You all know the waterfall behind King Brendan's Grotto?"

"Sure," Marit said, and Connor nodded.

"Behind the fall is a door in the rock—"

"No, there isn't," Marit cut in. "We've been there a hundred times."

Mistress Thule snorted. "Magicians unsealed it. Now listen. No one knows much—too many people scattered. Evacuation's still going on, and Lirwanis are busy at the Magic School and some o' the nobles' houses. But there are bands of brigands up here in the hills, making sport of killing any refugees they find. So we're to roam around, and if we find any of these bands, we pounce. Got it?"

"I like that plan," Marit said grimly. "Let's get to it."

They started walking up the pathway to where the horses had been left.

Mistress Thule stepped close to Connor. "My orders are to send any of the Royal Family to the falls."

"Can't I help you first?" Connor asked.

Mistress Thule grunted softly. "Like to have you along—you've got the best ears of any of us." She hesitated, then seemed to come to a sudden decision. "Here. Come with us, but first sign of trouble, you cut along to the Grotto. Got that?"

He nodded, and they walked in silence for a time. Connor looked at the muddy ground, thinking furiously. Though he trusted Mistress Thule, who had headed the palace guard for several decades, he couldn't tell her why he had "better ears" than anyone else. Did she suspect the truth?

Connor shook his head. His wayward magical sense provided him with a dim sense of direction and a vague awareness of mountain, cliff, and valley. He wondered how this walk in the dark was for the others.

A voice hailed them softly—the sentry posted to guard the rest of the patrol and the horses. Marit and Connor went to find their own mounts as Mistress Thule outlined the orders to the rest.

They started out, leading the horses under the thick trees. From time to time Connor heard a muffled curse as someone tripped in the darkness. Then one of the horses nickered, and Connor knew there was danger near.

He started to yell—and was drowned out by shouts and clashes of steel.

Greenish witch-light flared. Connor used it to mark his position, and then there was no time to think. A sudden buffet from behind made his ears ring. The shouts and clangs sounded distant. He kept his feet and turned to deal with the attacker, his arm responding with trained speed and force.

Then Marit cried out, his voice midway between a curse and a groan. Connor leaped at the silhouette bent over the boy, feinted, then stabbed under the attacker's arm.

The attacker gasped, fell, his sword flying. The man spasmed, then lay still.

23

I've killed him. Connor pulled his sword free, his mind and body completely numb with disbelief. Despite all his years of sword practice, and even a few fights, he had never actually killed anyone before.

He turned about, sword upraised, and the battle shifted abruptly. A whirlwind seemed to sweep upon them from behind, carrying away an enemy advancing on Connor, and for a moment he was left alone, his breathing harsh and his ears still ringing.

Then the Mistress's fingers gripped his shoulder. "Get him to safety."

Marit bumped up against Connor, whose throat closed at the sharp tang of fear-sweat mixed with the cloying scent of fresh blood.

"Go." And she gave him a shove.

Connor stumbled forward in the mud, Marit now leaning heavily against him. Somehow they made it away from the noise and confusion of the skirmish, then stopped. As Connor hastily cleaned his sword, Marit gasped, "Didn't know it would hurt so much! Got—to rest."

Connor said, "Soon. Hold on."

Marit's teeth clenched, but he stayed on his feet as they started moving again.

Connor led the way slowly. Away from the heat and noise of the fighting, his head cleared. He scanned the dark peaks, noting the peaceful stars glimmering between parting clouds, and suddenly his sense of direction oriented itself.

"Brendan's Grotto is this way."

The walk seemed endless, but at last Connor smelled the waterfall. Then he heard it, and they were feeling their way carefully down the cool, mossy path. Mist bathed their faces, they fumbled for the door, found it—and were in.

The cavern inside was crowded. Connor was beyond questioning how this mass of people had appeared. He recognized only a few, soot-begrimed nobles and servants who smelled of scorched cloth. A tall woman in healer-mage green suddenly emerged from the crowd and took Marit into her capable hands.

Connor watched them go, noting how Marit clutched his ruined arm to his side. The stone under Connor's feet seemed to ripple, and he grabbed at an outcropping of rock to steady himself.

"Your Highness." The voice seemed to come from far away. "Here's some listerblossom tea."

A cup was pressed to his lips. Steam bathed his cold face, and he breathed in the summer-sharp scent of herbs. Sipping, he ignored the scald and felt warmth and energy flow into his tired body.

Awareness returned, slowly. Taking his gloves off, he thrust them through his belt and grabbed the cup with both hands. Before him stood a palace servant, a boy near his own age, eyes dark with worry.

"Thanks, Porv. Where is the Princess?" Connor whispered hoarsely, apprehension chilling him.

"We don't know." Porv looked back along the tunnel, then said, "No one seems to know anything, or at least the ones who talk most don't make any sense. The Princess is missing." He added, "But so are the King and Queen and Duke Fortian. We hope they got away safely."

Teressa missing? Connor felt his heart pound sickeningly, and he leaned against the rough stone.

"We've got some food, if you'll step this way, Your Highness," Porv went on more formally.

Connor nodded, straightening up with an effort. Questions and answers began to flood his mind as he followed Porv up a narrow tunnel: *How long has this place been here, and why did no one talk of it? Obviously someone did know of it— Mistress Thule and the palace guard. I wonder if Verne and Astren know . . .*

A glimmer of red caught at the edge of his vision. He

glanced down at his ring and all thoughts of battle, exhaustion, and worry fled. It was the summons ring.

Teressa. "I have to find her."

Porv turned, eyes curious. "Pardon, Prince Connor? You spoke?"

Connor stopped. "Who is ahead?"

"The Duchess, Baroness Tamsal . . ."

Porv went on naming people, but Connor did not hear. Out of Meldrith's four royal families, there was only one Duchess: Carlas Rhismordith, his overbearing aunt. If she didn't want him to leave, she would order the servants to stop him—and she'd enjoy doing it.

"I must return to my patrol," Connor cut in quickly.

"But we have some food, and—"

Grabbing Porv's shoulder, Connor said, "Look. I thank you for the tea, and for the tidings. May I ask another favor?"

Porv's eyes widened, then he grinned suddenly. "You don't want Carp—ah, the Duchess to find you."

"Carping Carlas," Connor said with a twisted grin. It was not the first time he'd heard the nickname. "Right."

"I'm mum," Porv promised.

"Thanks. I'll return that favor some day."

Connor saluted, then made his way rapidly back down the tunnel.

When he had passed the sheet of water and was on the narrow path again, he peered down at the ring, moving it slowly in a circle.

The stone flared once, a flash of ruby that caused him to stumble forward at his fastest.

Tiredness was gone. Heart slamming in his chest, he threshed through unseen shrubs and ducked under branches outlined like ghosts against the half-clear sky. There was no trail, only the dimming or brightening of the stone that told him which direction to follow.

The journey seemed to take forever, and Connor's breath was burning the back of his throat when the ring suddenly glowed so brightly he knew Teressa had to be very near.

His right foot encountered a low stone step and he almost fell. Catching himself, he felt his way cautiously upward. Before long the familiarity of the stone steps made him recognize his surroundings.

He slowed a little, looking up at the ancient cedars that lined the worn stairway. He could see the steps in his mind's eye: white and glistening, made from a rare stone not found in Meldrith, ovals worn in the middle over hundreds of years. These days the place was called Rhis Garden, but it had been sacred long before the first Queen of Meldrith found it and made it a place of quiet and retreat for her descendants.

Somehow, time seemed to slow, and the terror of war was curiously distant, though Connor knew he was in no less danger than before. Maybe even more: Surely Andreus knew of this place and would search for it.

Thinking of Andreus reminded Connor of the man he had killed. Now, in the cool, peaceful night, the numbness that had cocooned him was gone. He remembered how his sword felt going between the man's ribs, how the man gasped in agony before he died.

Was the man really evil? Or just some foot soldier following orders?

Connor would never know. He hurried up the steps, as if to leave the memory behind.

As he climbed, invisible wind chimes tanged sweet, poignant notes and a breeze laden with spices and blossoms stirred his hair. A strange sense of sadness gripped him, yet his awareness widened and widened, until he was afraid to lift his gaze, afraid he just might see beyond the stars to a gate between worlds, and to watchers who would observe him and find him wanting.

At last, topping the final step, he walked into the old garden. A sense of peace enfolded him, and with it an almost overwhelming desire to bide here, hidden away from the war. But he looked at his ring, now glowing brightly indeed, and once again his steps quickened.

The ring led him through the garden, into the wild forest behind. Not too much farther he came upon a low cottage, set between a rocky cliffside and a wild thicket. Light glowed golden and welcoming through the tiny windows.

He stepped soundlessly onto the threshold and listened; and when he recognized two familiar voices, he thrust the door open, ready to give a glad cry. Then he froze, his hand still on the door.

The Princess looked shocked, her dark blue eyes wide and her long red-brown hair hanging down unkempt. Embracing her, his long limbs awkward, was Tyron.

For just a moment a terrible anger seared Connor, an anger he did not understand. Then he forced all emotion away and made himself walk inside, smiling at his best friend and at the Princess.

Only then did he see the tears on Teressa's cheeks, the pain in Tyron's face.

Teressa stirred and Tyron quickly dropped his arms. Teressa did not seem to notice. She stood, stepped forward, her hands out, and said softly, "Connor—my father and mother are dead."

A pang even fiercer than the one before flashed through Connor, burning like lightning. Only this time he knew what he felt: grief for his dead sister; shock; hatred for Andreus of Senna Lirwan. Then he found himself standing there with his arms around the Princess, and his awareness shifted to her. She was trembling and weeping soundlessly. But despite his own grief he smelled the familiar summer herbs with which she rinsed her hair.

Through them came Tyron's voice, insistent: "We have to plan."

Teressa pulled away, wiping her eyes. With a pale but determined face, she spoke. "Helmburi will return soon. We can plan better when we hear any news he brings. And if my uncle comes, he'll know even more."

"Tell me what happened," Connor said. His own voice sounded hoarse and far away.

"Please," Tyron added. To Connor, he said quickly, "I arrived just moments before you did."

"I was given a sleep elixir of some kind, in cider, by a girl I don't know," Teressa said. "Alif the stableboy was with her. They told me I was to go to the Rose Room. I made it to one of the secret passages, and there I fell asleep." She walked about the room, her hands gripped tightly. "When I woke up . . ."

She told the rest of her story quickly, in a flat voice. Twice she stopped with her lips pressed into a thin line, as if to hold back tears, but she managed to make it to the end of the story without breaking down.

Tyron sat quietly throughout. When she was done, he said, "That cup. What did you say was on it?"

Teressa blinked, her thoughts obviously distracted. "The cup?"

"The one you drank from," Tyron said. "Look," he added, shifting his gaze from the Princess to Connor, "I am more sorry than I can say, but we have to figure this out. Was Alif a plant of Andreus's? Or was this sleep elixir treachery from someone inside the castle?"

Teressa pressed her fingers to her forehead. "You are right. I must think . . ." She looked up. "I remember! It wasn't a house cup. That is, it did have the Rhis Family stars, but not our crowned sun. A bird—in flight—"

"Rhiscarlan," Tyron and Connor said together.

Teressa bit her lip. "Hawk Rhiscarlan. I never even thought of him. He must have thrown in with Andreus."

"I wonder," Tyron said. "I mean, if it was Andreus's plot, wouldn't he have had his minion stab you, or at least hand you over to the Lirwanis?"

"Sleep elixir . . . Rose Room," Connor said, trying to

think. "Isn't the Rose Room next to the room the magicians use for magic transfers?"

"Yes," Teressa said. "I never thought of that."

"If you were asleep, you wouldn't be able to resist a magic transfer. And if Hawk got ahold of you, he could use you as a bargaining counter against Andreus, who might otherwise try to make Hawk work for him. Didn't he rave on about his independence when he tried to kidnap you last year?"

Teressa exclaimed. "As if I could forget!"

Tyron snapped his fingers. "I'll bet Hawk somehow discovered Andreus's plot ahead of time, and this was his own power play." He looked thoughtful. "I wonder what Alif and his friend thought when they sneaked to the Rose Room to effect the transfer and plant the cup for Andreus to find—and you weren't there."

Teressa's pale face looked grim.

"But there's another thing that bothers me," Tyron said, "and I think we need to consider it right now." He looked from Teressa to Connor.

"Speak," Teressa said.

"Well, you said Duke Fortian gave Helmburi orders that if anything were to happen to your parents, he was to bring you to a place of safety. Yes?"

"It seems an added security measure," Teressa said. "And I am grateful, especially since I know how little my uncle likes me."

"But . . ." Tyron grimaced. "Ah, maybe I'm just too sour on him . . ."

Connor shook his head. "No. You're right. If the Steward was given special instructions, and told how to find Rhis Garden, then my uncle already had alternate plans. And one of those is probably to step in as regent. If he holds Teressa—purely for her safety—he will gain that position the more easily."

Teressa's face whitened. "He'll not rule through me," she said. "You're right, Tyron. I didn't think of that. Treachery!"

Tyron shook his head. "Fortian will see it as expediency." He stood.

"What I see," Connor pointed out, "is that when Helmburi brings him here, we'd best be long gone."

They stood there for a long moment, looking at one another. Connor could see in their faces the tiredness that he felt dragging at his own limbs, while from outside came the unwelcome hiss of steady rain.

Then Teressa grabbed up a long black cloak, her chin lifting. "Let's run," she said.

Chapter Five

Wren stood on the inn's broad hearth and raised her hands.
". . . and so the sea-kraken said to the shepherdess, 'I shall not give you your Prince back, I shall devour you instead!' " Wren quickly gestured with her hands as she muttered an illusion spell under her breath.

A monster's face appeared, three fireballs flaming from its mouth. The audience gasped. Wren gathered the fireballs and slowly started juggling them, adding three more. When she had the six fireballs spinning through the air, she went on with her story.

"So the shepherdess took from her pouch the six magic talismans . . ."

As she talked she glanced through the mesmerizing circle of fireballs at the faces beyond. There was no doubt that the patrons of the Two Badgers Inn, Porscan Square, Allat Los, liked her magic—and her stories.

"The sea-kraken disappeared with a mighty splash, and the waves cast upon the beach a great shell containing the sleeping Prince. The shepherdess kissed him . . ."

Wren clapped her hands and the balls exploded into showers of multicolored sparks that disappeared when they hit the floor. "And they all lived long and merry lives."

Drumming on the tables with silverware and crockery, the audience showed their approval.

Wren bowed to each side as she made her way to the back

counter, where her tall, grim-faced uncle poured out a glass of cold root cider.

A moment later, Wren's Aunt Niss bustled out from the kitchen, carrying a tray of steaming apple tarts. She gave Wren a merry smile, paused to tuck a wisp of unruly hair behind her ear, then whirled back into the kitchen. Wren watched, thinking about how she'd probably look just like Niss in a few years—short, round, and blue-eyed.

Except for this, Wren thought, flicking one of her braids behind her. Niss had brown hair, as Wren's own mother had had. But Wren's brown hair was streaked with pale locks, almost in stripes, and Wren had endured a lot of teasing about this during her days at the orphanage. *Aunt Niss said my father didn't have hair like this either,* she thought as she snagged a hot tart and a slice of meat pie and withdrew to a stool in a corner.

The metallic sound of tiranthe strings shimmered in the air, and the patrons quieted, turning toward the minstrel who was the next performer.

I wonder where my father is—if he's still alive. She wouldn't worry about that now. Tired and happy, Wren listened to the music, her gaze ranging high over the old beams in the common room. It was hard to believe that this inn had belonged to her mother—and might have been hers if she had not been lost as a baby and raised as an orphan in Siradayel. Wren glanced at her uncle. He'd not been pleased when she showed up so suddenly, looking for her missing family. He'd exacted a price before he'd let her meet her aunt Niss: Wren had had to sign the inn over to the Poths. She had done it quickly and without thought.

With plenty of time to think about it during this visit, she knew she had done the right thing. She'd worked hard to overcome her uncle's initial distrust of her, and her cousin Nad's jealousy. Two Badgers was now a home away from home where she could stay for a time, helping out with chores, entertaining the patrons, and contributing magic aids—like the glow-globes now lighting the stairwell. And when she was tired of the endless discussions of shipments and tallies and taxes and how distant problems affected prices, she could go back to the Magic School in Meldrith—and back to her studies.

Having finished off her pastry, Wren licked her fingers and stretched, feeling that life was indeed good. The only thing that could make it perfect—besides finding out if her father still lived—was if Teressa could somehow come with her on a visit.

Teressa—

Wren frowned, feeling a tickle of vertigo at the back of her mind. It brought back a memory of the bad dream she'd had two nights before. She'd meant to scry the Magic School and find out if everyone was all right, but then morning had come and with it the feeling that she was being silly. Teressa was surrounded by people who could look out for her welfare a lot better than one short magic prentice.

Certainly no one from school had tried to contact her, and she'd forgotten about the dream as the busy day sped by. She hadn't slept well since, which she attributed to being too excited about her chance to entertain the guests. She'd worked all day, in between chores, on her act.

But here again was the same feeling as in that dream—of unfinished business, of something not quite right.

Whirling about, Wren ran up the three flights to her small attic room—once her mother's room—and crossed to her narrow bed, where a bag of magic supplies sat on a bedside shelf. When she slid her hand into the bag, a reddish flicker glowing against her fingers was her first warning that something was wrong. The glow reminded her unpleasantly of fresh blood, and her fingers shook as she scooped out both her summons ring and her scry-stone.

She stared in dismay at the ring, wishing she hadn't taken it off that first day, when her aunt had asked her to help make piecrusts. Not used to wearing jewelry, she'd forgotten to put it back on again.

"Tess!" She cradled the scry-stone in her hands.

Her first instinct was to contact Mistress Leila—but she

was supposed to be still seeking aid at the Magic Council far away on another continent. *Mistress Ferriam is in charge of the Magic School,* Wren thought, summoning up an inner vision of the woman's face.

Nothing happened.

A chill prickled down Wren's neck. She tried harder.

Still nothing.

What now? She looked up, no longer seeing her cozy little room. Instead, her thoughts were far away in Meldrith. Who else should she try? Tyron was terrible at scrying. Who among the students?

"Laris." Wren summoned an image of Laris and was rewarded almost immediately with a contact.

"Wren! Close focus," the journeymage commanded.

Wren licked her lips. She didn't break concentration as she carefully constructed in her mind a wall around Laris, so that no other scryers could overhear them. It was a new lesson, and difficult, but she managed it without losing the contact.

"Is there a problem at the School?" Wren asked. "I had a bad dream—"

"We're here at the Free Vale, with Princess Teressa," Laris said flatly. "Wren, save your questions—even this close-focus contact is risky. I'll tell you why when you get here. Do you see the Designation pattern?"

Laris was very good at scrying. Though Wren had never been at the Free Vale magic transfer Destination, she could see very clearly the distinctive pattern of tiles on the floor of the Designation.

"Got it."

"Then transfer there. Remember, no one can transport inside the Vale—you'll be outside the border. But come inside quickly—there might be bad spells waiting." Then Laris closed off the contact.

Wren's heart thumped hard as she blinked away the feeling of dizziness left over from the scrying. Her fingers were shaky as she packed her things.

Downstairs, Wren found her aunt busy with two kitchen

helpers at the big preparations table. Niss smiled when she saw Wren and, tucking absently at another wisp of hair, left flour dotting her forehead and cheek as a result. But her smile faded quickly. "What is it, dear?"

Wren glanced at the other workers, then stepped close to her aunt. "I have to go. Trouble at home—" She swallowed in a suddenly dry throat. "In Meldrith. I have to help."

Niss did not argue or warn or cajole. She did not even ask what kind of trouble. She just nodded briskly and wiped her hands down her apron. "Shall I pack you some journey-food?"

"Won't need it. I have to go fast—by magic." Wren gave her aunt a fierce hug.

When she stepped back, Wren saw tears in her aunt's eyes, but Niss made a valiant attempt at a smile. "Be safe and well, my child. And we'll brew up some more root cider against your return."

Wren nodded, unable to make a sound.

Upstairs in her room, Wren clutched her bag tightly, picturing the Designation pattern of the Free Vale as she said the travel-spell.

A gray wind seemed to swirl around her, sweeping her into nothing—

And she blinked down at the floor, saw the tiles. "I did it!" she exclaimed, breathing deeply against the buzzing in her ears. Remembering stories told at the school about people who disappeared forever while trying transfers to Destinations they did not know, she felt a shiver of relief.

But right after it came the cold scrape of magic along her bones. Looking up, she saw a weird greenish fog forming. *That's got to be a very nasty spell, aimed at whoever transfers in,* she thought as she dashed out of the little cottage that housed the transfer Destination.

The air shimmered subtly before her. Wren flung herself through, recognizing the ancient border-protection spell. This time, she welcomed the worms-crawling-through-the-head sensation. It meant she was safely inside the Free Vale, and protected by magic older and more powerful than anything used by whatever villain threatened Meldrith now.

The pounding of feet behind her made her whirl around. Despite the fading light she easily recognized the tall, lanky youth in the shapeless tunic whose unkempt brown hair flapped in the wind. "Tyron!" Wren yelled.

Tyron's expressive, foxlike face beamed in relief. "You made it."

"Hoo! Almost not. Who put that spell out there?" She waved at the green fog, which was starting to dissipate.

"Andreus." Tyron's brown eyes narrowed with anger when he spoke the name, then widened. "Where were you? Why didn't the summons ring work?"

At Andreus's name, Wren felt cold, and not from the brisk wind scouring the grasses of the Haven. "I took my summons ring off. But then I had bad dreams and scryed Laris. She didn't tell me what's happened."

Tyron's long fingers gripped Wren's arm. The last rays of the disappearing sun highlighted his cheekbones and eye ridges, showing the tension there. "You'd better know the worst before we go in," he said softly. "The King and Queen are dead. So is Mistress Ferriam, and we think Master Falstan is either dead or captured."

"Tess?" Wren's voice came out in a squeak.

"She's fine," he said hastily. "So's Connor—and Laris and Kial and the prenties. We're all in that house yonder. It's a guesting house that the magicians here gave us."

"Temporary," Wren heard her own voice say, through the distance of shock. She felt an awful ache of grief for King Verne and Queen Astren, who had always been so kind to her.

"Nobody's slept much. We've been trying to plan. I'm so glad you're here," he added, drawing in a deep breath. "We really need you."

"I'm here," Wren said. "I'm home." But inside, the chill increased.

37

Chapter Six

*F*or a time they walked in silence. Tyron watched Wren look around the gentle valley, her light blue eyes blank. He knew she was not registering anything she saw. He hated to dump bad news like that, but it was better than Teressa having to do it.

"Hungry?" He touched Wren's shoulder.

She looked up at him, still with that queer blank look. At last she spoke. "Hungry?" Then she shook her head and managed to focus. "No. Ate at the inn."

"Well, there's plenty of food and hot apple cider—"

"Any root cider?"

"That too."

"I've room for that."

This is just what Teressa needs, Tyron thought. *Wren, with all her old spirit.*

"I take it Master Halfrid and the others aren't back," Wren said.

"And they can't get back, either. Andreus has really nasty ward-spells waiting for them if they come. So we don't dare try to contact them—just as well, right now, that they are busy wherever they are."

"So it's up to us?"

Tyron nodded grimly.

They trod up a flower-lined pathway to a long, low house with a thatched roof partly obscured by very old trees. Inside a big parlor room, Connor, Teressa, Kial, and Laris sat, finishing a meal.

"Wren!" Teressa ran forward and hugged her friend. Then she said to Tyron, half in reproach: "You didn't tell me!"

"I thought you were overdue for one *good* surprise," Tyron said.

Teressa took Wren by the shoulders, her face serious. "I have some bad news . . ." she started.

"Tyron told me," Wren said quickly. "I'm so sorry." She gave Teressa another hug.

Tyron saw Teressa's lips tremble, but just as the tears began she made a valiant effort and straightened up. "Then you'll know we have to start planning—right away. So Andreus can't do it to anyone else."

Wren dropped down on a hassock. "First, tell me what happened."

As Teressa told her story, Tyron joined Laris and Kial at the window. From there he could sit back and watch the others, for he was tired from sleepless nights—and from days filled with argument.

Connor leaned against a wall, arms folded as he listened to Teressa relate the now-familiar tale. He looked tall and strong and very competent—almost like a grown man.

Tyron blinked. When had Connor gotten so tall? He stretched his own long legs out in front of him. They were suddenly unfamiliar, as if they belonged to someone else. Those weren't the legs of a stick-thin boy, like that brand-new prentice, Jao, sitting so small and scared with the other prenties in the kitchen. *I haven't noticed Connor growing because I've gotten tall myself.* Yet inside, Tyron felt as young as Jao. *Except for the last few days, when I've felt a hundred years old.*

". . . so Connor managed to find three horses for us, and we rode the rest of the way without any further trouble. And that's my story," Teressa said. She looked up at Connor. "You want to tell Wren what happened to you?"

"There's little to tell," Connor said. "We were coming back from border patrol and tangled with brigands. We saw Andreus. Marit was hurt, and then the summons ring brought me to Teressa and Tyron."

39

"What about the Magic School?" Wren asked.

"I'll tell her," Laris said. "Wren, we used some of your spells . . ."

Tyron watched the Princess as Laris talked. Suddenly she looked different too. Though her large eyes and the long braid of auburn hair were familiar, her proportions had changed. She was no longer the gawky, round-faced girl who had reappeared from the orphanage where she'd been hidden for years. She sat quietly now, in total concentration, her expressive eyes darkening.

"The School burned?" Wren repeated, her voice going high. "All of it?"

"I don't think all of it can burn," Tyron said quickly.

"Not the stone portions," Laris put in. "And you know, it's been around an awful long time. I wouldn't be surprised if there weren't some sort of protection spells on it that might have been activated."

"Rotten, rotten, *rotten,*" Wren exclaimed, crossing her arms. "Those double-dirty, squashheaded, maggot-crawling rotters!"

"This is why we have to act, and soon," Teressa said briskly, looking in turn at each person in the room. "We have to strike back, before Andreus and his villains ruin Meldrith."

"What can *we* do?" Wren asked. "I'm ready, but I don't see how our little group can take on an entire army—and live past a day, that is."

"True," Teressa said. "We have to find our own army. That's my job."

"But you can't—" Laris protested.

"You have to—" Wren began.

"I can, and I will," Teressa said. "I've been thinking about it a lot. Especially at night," she admitted with a wry smile. "And we've been talking about it a lot." She sent a straight look across the room at Tyron. "What I see are two battles ahead of me. One with the Lirwanis, and another at home. Though I'm still a princess until I'm crowned, I have to act like

40

a queen. This means I have to convince people that I can rule the kingdom." Teressa's face changed subtly as she spoke. Tyron wondered if anyone noticed the slight falter when she said "kingdom." Then he noticed Wren wince in sympathy. *Wren knows what it is costing Teressa to hide her grief.*

How like her father Teressa looked now, chin high, brow slightly creased, he thought. She had inherited her father's strength of will. Then she smiled, and that brought the Queen to mind, for Teressa, like her mother, did not willingly speak her thoughts. But Tyron had finally learned her other language, the one she spoke with eyes and hands.

You will one day be the Queen's Magician, Halfrid had said. *You will need to know Teressa as a person as well as a ruler, for you must be strong where she is weak, and where she is strong you will have to be wise.*

Forcing his attention back to the present, Tyron heard Teressa say, "My uncle Fortian already controls whatever remains of the Scarlet Guard, and the palace guards, plus his own Blues. I know he won't turn them over to me. What I plan to do is raise the rest of the country—the ordinary folk, to whom my uncle would never think of turning. If I'm fast enough, maybe I can form my own army, and then I can return to face my uncle."

Wren had been frowning as she listened. "Then he can't pretend you're too young to rule, right?"

"Exactly," Teressa said grimly. "Assuming he lets me be crowned, I won't have him as regent. I hate him—though that wouldn't matter, if he were a good governor. He's not. I saw the evidence myself on this last trip."

Wren's blue gaze suddenly pinned Tyron. "But you don't like her plan."

"It's not that—" Tyron began to protest.

"But you don't. I can tell," Wren went on, adding, "when you get that burr-up-the-nose look I know you're disapproving of something."

The magic prentices laughed. Tyron glanced at Teressa

41

and was relieved when she smiled. "It's not the army part of the plan that bothers me," he said. "It's the sneaking-around part. I think she ought to go back to Cantirmoor and face Fortian Rhismordith down. If she doesn't, I'm afraid either one of two things will happen."

"One—he'll catch up with her somehow?" Wren asked.

"Yes," Tyron said. "And it'll look bad to the rest of the country if the Princess is running from her own side. The other problem is that if the Scarlet Guard does manage to get rid of the Lirwanis, then it will look like Teressa ran away when trouble began. That would seem even worse than running from your own side."

Teressa shook her head. "That's the risk I have to take. Everything in war is a risk, isn't it? In the meantime, I think it a bad idea to face my uncle without a strong army at my back. He won't listen to me otherwise. I think he wants more than anything to be king."

Wren said, "How will you gather a whole army and be sure that some of them aren't spies? You don't know everyone in the kingdom."

"But I do know a lot of loyal folk," Teressa said. "I know the ones I can trust. I'll ask them to find volunteers from among their own people."

"Meantime, what about the Lirwanis? Let them do what they want?"

"Well, I hope my uncle will be doing his best against them with the Scarlet Guard, because even though he's greedy and mean, he's not a coward. He'll be fighting to gain and hold the capital. He won't bother with the rest of the country, which is where we'll be. And as for the enemy, we'll need a band willing to turn the Lirwanis' tactics against them."

"You mean, like those brigands?" Wren asked. "Attacking and burning the Lirwanis' camps? What good will that do?"

"If they are busy chasing after their attackers, it might delay the consolidation of Andreus's power," Teressa said. "I thought that out last night; I remembered reading about similar tactics in a book on Fil Gaen's history."

"Do you want us doing that?" Wren looked dubious.

Teressa said firmly, "Connor will take charge of that part. We'll start out in a big group just until we reach Rhismoor, then we'll split into two."

Connor glanced up briefly, then returned to studying the floor. Tyron realized that they had settled the plans in private, which made him feel odd. He also realized that Connor was not completely happy with the decision. *But he hasn't talked to me about it. Why?*

"What about us magicians?" Wren asked.

Teressa turned to Laris. "I hoped that you would come with me, for I will have great need of your communication skills."

Laris flushed with pleasure. "I'll be glad to."

Teressa looked up at Kial. "Would you go with Connor's group and act as their healer? I hope they won't need you, but . . ."

"I will," Kial said. "But what about our prentices?"

"Let's find out what they want to do. We can certainly use them." Teressa turned to Tyron then. "I wish you would come with me. I know you don't like my plan, but I'll need your help."

Tyron shook his head, hating the argument. Hating his own doubts. "I'm not against your plan. Except for the part about the Duke. I think we need to work against Andreus's magic and not just his army."

Teressa flexed her hands, then buried them under her skirt. She was angry again, though her face did not show it. "You'll only get yourself killed, and maybe to no purpose. Perhaps I don't understand the importance of magic theory and practice, but what I see is that we need to fight Andreus now."

Wren looked from one to the other, her face serious. "What's this?"

"My own plan," Tyron said. "I feel someone ought to go

43

to Senna Lirwan—'someone' being me—and raid Andreus's library. See if we can find out his secrets. Then we can weaken his magic with his own spells."

"But no one can get into Senna Lirwan!" Wren exclaimed. "Now, I mean. We did once, but don't you think he's figured out how, and laid a lot of nasty traps against anyone trying it again?"

"Probably," Tyron replied. "But once I get to Edrann there'll be less danger than last time, because Andreus won't be there. He's busy ruining things here."

Wren chewed her lip, frowning.

Silence fell. Tyron realized Teressa was waiting to hear Wren's opinion, as if hers might be the deciding vote.

Finally Wren looked up. "I think you're right," she said at last. She turned toward Teressa. "So are you. But wouldn't it be better to avoid battles if we can? We haven't enough people for them. Or the arms. Trying to undo Andreus's magic seems the neatest way to solve this mess, if we can do it. So while you are gathering your army, which is going to take time, we can try. Am I right?"

"Three of you think so," Teressa said softly, her face blank, her hands still hidden.

"But." Wren sat up a little straighter, as if bracing herself. "I think I'm the one to go. Tyron, Tess needs you here."

Everyone laughed, and it broke the tension that Tyron had felt building.

Wren put her hands on her hips. "So you think it's funny?"

Connor put out his hands. "Peace, Wren. It's just that— when we talked about this earlier—somehow we knew you'd volunteer for the nastiest and most dangerous job."

"Well, if it needs doing—"

Tyron looked across at the Princess, who smiled at him at last. "Well, if you really think it might work," Teressa said to Wren, "then I won't argue anymore. But, Wren, we already have a job for you, almost as nasty."

"Uh, oh." Wren groaned. "If it's to tackle Andreus personally—*much* as I'd *love* to do it—"

Everyone laughed again.

"Wren," Teressa said, kneeling down next to her. "You can say no, for this one will have its own dangers."

Wren looked up at Tyron. "Let's have it."

"You remember what Teressa said about that cup of sleeping potion?"

"The Rhiscarlan device on the side?" Wren said. Then she gasped. "You can't mean you want me to go find that stinker of a Hawk!"

Teressa smothered a laugh at the word "stinker" and nodded.

Tyron felt no urge to laugh. Though Hawk was only a couple of years older than Tyron, he was a very powerful magician, and Tyron did not like to remember having been his prisoner.

"*Ghack!* Why?" Wren exclaimed, looking from one to another.

"Well, we can't prove that the cup was his," Tyron said, "but after our experiences with him, don't you think it's the sort of thing he'd do?"

"But if he tried to kidnap you, Tess, why should we talk to him at all?"

"Because the more we looked at the circumstances, the more we realized he was acting independently of Andreus. This seems to suggest that he's on his own. And," Tyron said with deep meaning, "a stinker he may be, but wouldn't you rather he be on our side than the Lirwanis'?"

Wren looked from one to the other. "Hawk Rhiscarlan," she said, holding her nose. "And to think that just this morning I was sleeping in my room at the inn, where there are no problems worse than tariffs and stale bread." She added with feeling, "I'll do it. But I'd rather he turned into a toad and hopped away."

45

Chapter Seven

*W*ren and Teressa had breakfast alone the next morning.
At first Wren tried to make Tess smile by describing some
of the odd customers at her aunt's inn. Teressa did smile, but it
was a polite kind of smile, and every time Wren stopped talking, Teressa's gaze went distant.

Finally Wren put her spoon down and touched Teressa's
wrist. "Talk."

Teressa shook her head. "It's nothing . . ." But then she bit
her lip and said, "Oh, Wren, I'm scared, and not just of the
Lirwanis, though that's a lot of why I can't sleep at night. It's
facing our own people that worries me most—commanding
them. Or trying to. I don't know if it's because I spent all those
years in the orphanage, or if it would have happened anyway,
but I've never really felt like a princess. And I certainly do not
feel like a queen. I mean, why should I be one? Just because I
happened to be born a Rhisadel?"

Wren opened her mouth to reassure Teressa, then closed
it. Teressa did not want to be told that she looked the part, that
she was smart, that her parents had believed in her. She knew
those things.

Thinking hard, Wren lifted her cup of liesberry tea and
breathed the sweet steam. She was going to leave on her own
mission as soon as they were done eating. If she was to help
Tess, it had to be right now.

Wren said slowly, "You didn't talk to your parents about
that?"

46

"I did, one time. To my father." Teressa's lip trembled when she mentioned the King. She pressed her mouth into a firm line, then continued. "He told me once that, when he was small, he had gotten mad when he realized he couldn't be a stablehand. He said he hated keeping his clothes clean and sitting still during long council meetings, and he especially hated the parties! He liked horses and envied the boys and girls in the stable. So he told the King to pick one of his cousins as heir so that he could work in the stable. Because a prince ought to be free to do what he wants."

"The old King must have loved that," Wren said, remembering what she'd heard about his legendary temper.

Teressa smiled wryly. "Punished him severely. Bread and water for two weeks. And he had to attend every function but was forbidden to speak." She toyed with her food. "Papa said he learned to keep his opinions to himself. Then he told me that if I had any similar feelings, he'd make me work in the stable a week and see how I liked it. He said that after several long days of mucking, and pitching, and carrying, and more mucking, I'd be glad to go back to what I was trained to do."

Wren helped herself to another muffin. "Then what he was saying was, if a stableboy wanting to be a prince got a week's worth of prince duties, he might be glad to go back to what he was trained for as well—right?"

"That's right," Teressa said. "I didn't know how to answer it, really, except to say that I still felt the same way. So I was silent."

Wren dropped her knife. "I know where you two missed each other."

"Where?" Teressa looked hopeful.

"Well, your father always knew he was a prince; he just wanted out. Now, take me. You know I was trained at the orphanage for pottery, and I was getting to be *al*most adequate, but I hated it, always had hated it, and always would. I wasn't born to be a potter. Neither was I born to be a magician. You might say I found it, it didn't find me."

47

Teressa smiled. "What I remember was you changing your mind every week about what you would rather be doing!"

"Except it always had to have traveling and adventure in it," Wren said, grinning.

"So you think I should give up this pretense of being Queen? If so, what would I do?" Teressa's smile faded. "And who is to take my place—besides Uncle Fortian, who would just love to be King?" she finished bitterly.

Wren's heart hammered. Was that what she meant? Had she just hurt her best friend at the worst time of her entire life? She took a huge bite out of her muffin, thoughts chasing through her head. At last she said, "Halfrid told us that good magicians don't think about what magic powers can do for them, they think about what good they can use their powers for. It seems to me a queen who asks herself *why* she should be a queen—what she can do to be a good one—is not such a bad thing."

"I see. So the question inside can be a good thing?"

Wren nodded vigorously. "Makes you think about what you're doing."

Teressa said, "Maybe if I can convince myself, I can convince others."

Greatly relieved, Wren picked up her dishes. "Time to thank Kial's prenties for that breakfast and apologize for not taking my turn in the kitchen." And with a glance out the window at the sky, she added, "Maybe they'll feel sorry for me and give me extra muffins for my journey."

Teressa also picked up her dishes. "They won't let me help in the kitchen," she said. "I used to like kitchen chores at the orphanage. Even Connor got a turn yesterday, but me . . ."

They mean well, but they're making her feel worse, Wren thought, leading the way. She resolved to speak to the others before she left.

Over her shoulder, she said, "They're probably afraid you'll break the magicians' dishes and we'll all get turned into toadstools," and her reward was Teressa's laugh.

After Teressa went out of the kitchen, Wren exchanged a

few quick words with Kial about her. Then Wren began a search for Tyron. All over the house, everyone was busy doing at least two chores at once, but when she found Tyron, he was just standing at a window in a small upper room, looking eastward.

She had to say his name twice before she got his attention, and when he turned, his slanty brown eyes were remote. She hesitated for a moment. Was he angry? At her?

"You did say last night we should talk about how I'm to approach Hawk Rhiscarlan . . ." she began.

Tyron blinked. "What's that?" he asked. "Oh, yes. Our good friend Hawk."

He's not angry, he's worried. Wren advanced into the room, feeling that things were normal again. Tyron, she knew, was a champion worrier.

"Did you find out if Idres Rhiscarlan is in the Haven?" Wren asked.

"That was the first thing I did when we got here," Tyron said. "As usual, no one would tell me anything. I got the feeling, though, that she comes and goes."

"Then she's watching the war. Or at least she's watching Andreus."

Tyron nodded. "We know she really loathes Andreus. She may not want to help any of us, but she *won't* help him. I just don't know if she'll help Hawk—who is a relative of hers, after all."

Wren thought of the tall woman with her long midnight hair and cool demeanor. "She's not the type to be sentimental."

"No," Tyron said. "As for Hawk, I learned a little about him the time I was his prisoner. Don't bargain with him, Wren. He might help us if it amuses him. Teressa thinks so, anyway. Make it quick, and if he says no, just leave."

"That's a mighty long walk for what may be nothing. But at least I don't have to go to Senna Lirwan." She held her nose. "What about after?"

"Find us with your summons ring. Don't wear it openly,

though. Last night Laris scryed old Master Kobel at Arakee-by-the-Lake. He says they are crowding up with refugees. The Lir-wanis are riding through villages and destroying food storage and houses, and they have special orders to seek out magicians. So you'll have to get rid of that." He pointed at her tunic. "Laris found trunks of castoff clothes in the attic, and the magicians did say to help ourselves to what we needed. Any-way, I hope I'll be back before you. I'll transfer to the Lake Destination and go up the mountains from there."

"I can always return by magic, if—"

"Don't," Tyron said. "Not unless Hawk has a clear Desig-nation. Don't try an outside transfer. You don't know what nasty ward-traps Andreus has waiting for just that."

"I'll remember," Wren said. "Speaking of traps, *can* I get out of the Haven? Remember that terrible magic when I ar-rived yesterday?"

"That was just at the Designation. Andreus hasn't had time to ward the entire Haven border. I am not even sure he can. I think you'll be all right, though I'd go to the south end before leaving."

"All right," she said. "I think we've covered everything."

"Good luck." He held out both hands.

"And to you," she said, clasping them, then turning away.

Laris was already in the attic, poking around in the ornate trunks and old boxes lined neatly against the eaves. She greeted Wren, holding up a fabulous gown embroidered with gem-stones that glittered in the cold blue light of a glow-globe. "From the looks of these clothes," she said, "some of Mel-drith's history has passed through this Haven between chap-ters."

Wren looked down at a trunk carved with flying beasts, the wood so old it was black and grainless. "I hope it's not just toff clothes in those chests. I can't see slogging down the road in a silk gown."

"Me, either," Laris said. "Practical things over there." She pointed to a corner. "I was just trying to imagine . . . well, what it must be like to wear one of these things in a palace. You'll think that's pretty stupid," she added hastily.

"No, I don't, because I wondered too, right until I visited Tess and we went to parties. The dancing is fun, but the rest—" She shrugged, not wanting to say anything against some of Teressa's high-born but snobbish relatives. "People standing around in fancy clothes, eating, drinking, and jabbering about either love or politics—both being about as fun as a mudslide, in my opinion."

Laris sighed, carefully refolding the gown. "I think I'll keep my dreams, thank you."

Wren made her way to the trunks Laris had pointed out, hoping that some of the unknown historical personages had been short and round.

Moments later she had two sets of clothes laid aside, both traveling tunics suitable for boys or girls. One was made from a fabric little seen in Meldrith, heavy but very soft. Tiny leaves and flowers had been embroidered by patient fingers along the hem, the wide cuffs, and down either side of the lacings in front. Someone had loved that tunic, Wren thought, holding it up. The elbows were worn thin, and one side as well, where a pouch had hung. *Or maybe a sword.*

She felt strange changing out of the brown tunic that had been her uniform since she became a magic student. As she pulled on the loose trousers and belted the embroidered tunic over them with her prentice sash, she felt stranger still, thinking that she might be wearing some famous person's clothes.

At least with my old mocs and my cloak on, I feel like me, and not someone else, she thought, packing up her things.

Then it was time for good-byes. She found everyone but Teressa and Connor in the kitchen, the stable, or the parlor, all working. But she would not leave without saying good-bye to her best friend.

She opened door after door in all the rooms, until in an

51

isolated corner under the slanting roof she found Teressa and Connor. They stood before a window, talking earnestly. Wren took a step in and was about to open her mouth, just as Connor grasped both of Teressa's hands. Neither of them noticed her.

"I want more than anything to help you, but *not* as an army commander."

"*Why* not, Connor?" Teressa asked, looking earnestly up into his face. "You're the best of any of us."

Connor shook his head. "Good at quarterstaff and adequate with a sword, and I've learned something about how a patrol works. But an army?"

"So what am I to do, then?" Teressa asked.

"Send to Siradayel for my half-brother, Rollan. Or wait, because someone will come forth who can lead. I just know I'm not qualified. I'm sorry."

Teressa sighed, then leaned against Connor, who stroked her hair.

They don't know I'm here. Embarrassed, Wren started to back out, but the floor creaked.

Connor and Teressa jumped apart, Connor flushing up to the ears. But Teressa just bit her lip, her expression difficult to interpret.

"Um. I'm leaving," Wren said, fumbling for the door latch.

"Wait, Wren, we want to see you off," Teressa said.

All the way down the stairs, Wren talked about the clothes she'd found, babbling to keep her friends from feeling as embarrassed as she did. Once or twice Connor smiled, but Teressa seemed preoccupied.

Outside, Wren squinted at the sky and tightened her cloak about her. Lumpy iron-colored clouds glowered from horizon to horizon, and an icy wind fingered her braids, promising worse weather to come.

Teressa hugged her. "Are you sure you won't take one of our mounts?"

Wren shook her head. "I'm likely to find someone to ride with eventually, and it'd be harder on your group to have to double up. For now I'll walk." She added in a fierce whisper, "You just be careful!"

"Be well and safe, Wren," Teressa murmured, looking worried.

Wren shrugged her heavy knapsack on and said with as much cheer as she could muster, "I'll be sure to give Hawk your warmest cousinly greetings."

Teressa sniffed. From behind her, though, came a laugh from Connor. "Give him mine, too, Wren."

"And mine," Tyron called from the stairwell. "Why not?"

Everyone laughed at Tyron's joke, and Wren set out down the pathway.

As Tyron had guessed, there were no magic traps at the Haven border.

Wren bent into the tearing wind, thinking about the last time she had set out on this road, with Tyron, their destination Senna Lirwan. They'd had no idea then what that journey would entail. This time, she thought she knew.

Though I can't believe Andreus doesn't expect anyone to try anything against him in his own land, Wren thought, feeling a chill that cut deeper than the wintry wind.

The dull thud of hoofbeats brought her attention back. She moved quickly to the side of the road, almost slipping in a mud patch. A group of tired horses trotted by, bearing dispirited-looking people who clutched bags and rolls of belongings.

Refugees. Once again, this time by sheer contrast, Wren was reminded of her last journey. She and Tyron had been almost alone on the road, the season early spring. Tyron had not known it then, but the senior magicians had let him go as a kind of test. Now, he was in charge of the other magicians—all the decisions falling on his shoulders. *He must be terribly worried,* Wren thought.

And then her thoughts skipped back to the scene she had inadvertently witnessed between Connor and Teressa. Romance? And at the start of a war! She groaned as drops of rain spattered her forehead and wrist. Would this romance stuff hurt her friendship with Teressa? Pulling her cloak more tightly around her, Wren squinted up at the clouds. Would it hurt her friendship with Connor?

Hoofbeats interrupted her thoughts again. Someone galloping, she realized, and ducked behind a line of roadside shrubs.

The riders flashed by, two and two, mud covering whatever colors and devices they might have been wearing.

The rain increased steadily and, as the afternoon wore on, turned sleety. Wren hunched into her cloak, feeling the tingle of her cloak's magic working to repel the water. Where the hood blew back and the cloak flapped open, Wren's face and legs were numb with cold, but the rest of her was reasonably dry. *I'm glad I restrengthened the wet-wards on my moccasins and mittens and knapsack,* she thought, clutching the cloak even tighter around her.

As she leaned into the driving wind, she forgot about her friends and concentrated on staying on her feet. Several times more, she heard horses approach. Usually the riders sped by, but once the noise was a coach, driven as swiftly as the galloping horses, and later a laden wagon with two shrouded figures atop, swaddled to the eyes.

Wondering if she could get a ride, Wren lifted a hand and shouted, but whether the wind snatched her words away too quickly or the people simply ignored her, she did not know. They passed on and were soon swallowed by the gathering gloom, the cart wheels creaking alarmingly. So she plodded on.

Darkness had nearly fallen when she began scanning the rough countryside for somewhere to camp. It would be a miserable night unless she could find some cave or thick copse of trees to shelter under. Then again she heard the thud of hoof-beats.

This time the rhythm was slower. As she squinted into the steady rain, she saw the flicker of light through the droplets, like a sudden swarm of fireflies. The cool, steady blue light of glow-globes illuminated the puddled road, and a few moments later, a covered wagon with two drivers came into view.

To her surprise, as soon as the wagon drew alongside her a female voice clucked to the horses, and they stopped, their heads low.

"Refugee?" a voice called out.

Was she? *I'd be an idiot to announce that I'm on a mission for the Princess.*

"Yes," she called. And under her breath, "From this weather, if nothing else."

"Come up," another voice called, also female; but this one was old. "We'll trade you a ride for any news you know."

Wren clambered up on the box and sank gratefully onto the hard wooden seat. "Thanks," she said. "I'd forgotten what real comfort felt like."

The older one cackled. "How long you been walkin'?"

"Oh, about forty years," Wren joked.

They both laughed as the driver clucked to the horses and, with a lurch, the wagon pulled forward again.

"We're from Keet," the old woman said. "Cursed stone-bones fired the Baroness's house four days gone, then started on the villages. So we grabbed what we could before they could get to us, and here we are."

"Stonebones?" Wren repeated, delighted with the image.

"Them Lirwanis in their gray tunics," the driver said. She didn't sound much older than Teressa. "Look like stone, hearts of stone. So anyhow, Brother went to find the Princess or the Duke and offer to fight. Papa as well. Mama stayed to defend the village."

As Wren listened to this news, she wondered what she ought to say. She'd become practiced at keeping secrets—not just magical ones. She'd even learned to keep quiet about her newfound relations and the inn. Except for Connor, Tyron, and Tess, no one at the School knew that she had a family.

Not that anyone at the School was untrustworthy. *But as a magician you are going to run into trouble,* Tyron had told her soon after her last adventure. *The less your enemies can find out about you, the less they can use against you.*

In three years, Wren had never found out anything about Tyron's own family—or even if he had one. Secrets started right at home.

"How about you, young one?" the grandmother asked. "What's your tale?"

It was always possible that they were Lirwani spies. Far more likely that they were exactly what they said. But anything Wren told them would get told again and again over firesides over the next days. And eventually unfriendly ears would be listening.

"I'm a prentice," Wren said. "Lirwanis burned our place, so I've been sent south to seek help."

"Got a good guild southward, eh?" the driver asked. "Like the wheelwrights. Four of us are wheelwrights."

"What do ye do?" the grandmother asked.

"I've been trained in potterymaking," Wren said, remembering those long, boring days at the kilns when she was at the orphanage in Siradayel.

They rode in silence for a time. Wren, aware suddenly of her growling stomach, pulled her knapsack around front and dug through it. She pulled out one of the muffins, carefully wrapped in a napkin. It was cold and had hardened a little, but it tasted wonderful.

A few bites later she was conscious of her fellow travelers. Neither had said a word, but she felt their interest. Hoping she wouldn't end up running out of food before she got anywhere, she completely unwrapped the napkin and produced the rest of the muffins.

"Hungry?" she asked, holding them out.

They hesitated only a moment, then the grandmother said, "Journeycakes and carrots get mighty old after four days." And a moment later, she added through a mouthful, "Very fine baking here. Fine indeed."

The driver chimed in, "Our thanks to you, Traveler. If you don't mind, I'll just save these last two for the young ones." She hesitated. "Listen, you know aught of horses?"

"Some," Wren said.

"We're going to find us some cover soon and tend these here horses. You just crawl in under the flap, and mind you don't squash the two little ones a-sleeping on the bags. Tomorrow you can spell us with the driving—we're going far as Hroth Falls."

"Right on my way," Wren said happily.

Chapter Eight

Connor opened his eyes the moment he felt the touch on his shoulder.

"Your watch," Kial whispered apologetically.

Connor sat up, blinking away grogginess. He grabbed sword and belt, clutching his cloak around him against the bitter cold. Then, pacing carefully through the starlit darkness to a flat space beyond the perimeter of the camp, he forced himself to drop the cloak and pull his sword free of its sheath. The faint *shear*ing noise of metal sliding fingered its way down his back, making him feel colder even than the air.

Deliberately emptying his mind of thought, he began swinging the sword back and forth from hand to hand. When he whirled into the first steps of the practice ritual called the Shadow Dance, he began to warm up at last.

It took concentration to do it correctly, and as Mistress Thule had always said, there was no point in doing it unless one did it right. Still, he was on watch, so he had to keep eyes and ears sharp.

Thus he was aware of a figure walking toward him from the camp, a silhouette darker than the landscape. Somehow he knew it was Teressa.

His heart warmed. It seemed impossible to him that out of all the fellows at Court she liked him best, a landless younger son, and a kind of relative as well. Not that they'd talked about their feelings—she seemed as shy that way as he was. In fact,

58

they were a lot alike. But when others weren't looking, her hand sought his.

He laughed as he finished his Shadow Dance. The cold no longer mattered. He felt strong and sure of victory. How could they not win? They had right on their side, and Teressa cared for him.

"What are you laughing about?" Teressa whispered, coming into the clearing. She was still just a silhouette against the horizon, her outline blurred by a wisp of fog drifting among the trees. But he could feel her smiling.

"Because I think we'll win. I know it," he said.

She sighed. "Oh, I hope you are right."

The smile had gone out of her voice. Connor felt some of his joy leach away. He buckled on his sword belt, then crossed the clearing to sit on a fallen log. Teressa came around it and sat down next to him, her hands pressed tightly between her knees. "What is it?" he said.

The darkness hid her expression, but he could hear the tightness in her voice. "So much can go wrong!"

"True. So why worry? You've a good plan. You ought to be sleeping so you'll be sharp tomorrow. If we're fast, we'll reach Rhismoor by noon."

"I'm worried because I'm starting a war," she said.

"You can't start it," Connor said. "Andreus already did. You're just giving your people the chance to fight back."

"My people," she whispered.

Connor hesitated, guessing at what lay behind her words. He'd heard Verne Rhisadel talk about this very thing, just once. *If any Meldrithi citizen dies under her leadership, will she blame herself?* he thought. *Verne called it "the price of kingship," and he said he wanted to leave his daughter a peaceful kingdom so she would never know its cost.*

What could he offer as comfort? *Nothing,* he thought. *It's the reason why I can't command any army. The price is too high.*

"Teach me to use a sword," she whispered.

Caught by surprise, he hesitated. What could she possibly learn in time to be useful? Then he understood. *It'll feel like purposeful action, which she needs right now.*

"All right," he said. "Night is a good time, actually. If you can't see, you'll learn the right grip and stance the faster."

He pulled his sword free again and pressed the hilt into her fingers. Her wrist bent, and her hand dropped with the heavy sword, but she grunted with effort and forced it up again.

"Now, here's where we begin," he said . . .

Light limned the distant trees when they stopped. He could see Teressa's pale face and the determined jut of her chin, and despite the chilly air her brow was damp.

She thanked him gravely and walked back toward the camp, her hands beating impatiently at her dew-stained skirts. She had learned half the Shadow Dance. As Connor watched her he realized, with regret, that he'd let her work too long, that she would be sore before the day was over.

But Teressa never voiced any complaint as the dawn gradually changed into a cloudy day. Everyone in the camp roused, working together to prepare food, eat it, then pack what was left for the day's ride. Connor scoured his plate and spoon clean and put them into his saddle roll.

His horse tossed her head and nuzzled his shoulder. Looking furtively around him, Connor laid his hand against the mare's skull and listened to her thought-images as she snorted. This was his single reliable magical talent, to be able to understand birds and animals.

The mare's mind was on sweet grass. Jao, the smallest magic prentice, had worked with horses before coming to the Magic School, so he was in charge of the mounts. He was evidently very good at his job. Despite long rides, the horse was fit and content.

"Ready to ride?" A voice behind Connor broke into his thoughts.

Connor backed away from the mare's head. No one except Wren, Teressa, and Tyron knew about his talent for communicating with animals. Connor was unwilling to let anyone else find out.

Kial approached, leading his horse. "Lucky us," he said cheerfully, "that Ruen grew up in a wayside inn before he turned magic prentice. That oatmeal was the best I've ever tasted."

Connor nodded. "Who would have thought to put wild nuts into it?"

"Stretches it out," Laris said practically, appearing on the other side. "I just hope we'll be able to find supplies at all, once winter hits in earnest."

"Oh, we will," Kial said, still cheery. "Even if we have to steal the breakfasts right out of the graybacks' spoons."

"Except with our luck, all the Lirwanis eat for breakfast would be boiled turnips with fried crickets," Laris said. "I'm more worried about our mounts." She gave hers a pat, then added to Connor, "Some of these School horses are old, and none of them have ever been trained in any kind of war skills."

"Mount up," Teressa called, her voice clear and carrying. "Let's see if we can outrun this coming rain." She pointed to the north.

They climbed into their saddles and started the day's ride.

Connor stayed in the lead, with his small band of hastily trained magic prentices right behind him. They were supposed to serve as scouts, which none of them really knew how to do. Connor used his listening skills to find out from passing birds if any large parties were on the roads ahead. It had worked so far, but with winter threatening, birds were scarcer each day.

Rain started at midmorning, soft at first but quickly turning into a downpour. An abrupt shift in wind brought a steady pelting that abated a little before noon. They arrived on a ridge above Rhismoor, soggy but still high in spirit. The clouds were moving eastward, leaving a clear view of a town nestled in the gentle valley below.

Connor scanned Rhismoor carefully, looking for signs of fighting.

Drawing her horse up beside Connor's, Teressa sat tall and straight, her face determined under her crown of wet braids. As if steeling herself, she lifted her chin and said, "Shall we go find the town Elders and start our army?"

Kial led a cheer, and the horses began trotting down the road.

Just as they sighted the bridge into town, Connor heard the muffled thunder of hoofbeats. A few moments later, a cavalcade swept out through the open gate, two by two in neat formation. Pale sunlight glittered on jeweled hilts and brooches holding rich cloaks in place. Connor stared in dismay at the thin, sharp-faced leader.

"It's Garian," Teressa muttered in disbelief, her hands tightening on her reins. "How'd *he* find us?" Her mount sidled, ears laid back.

Garian Rhismordith put a gloved hand up and his riders halted. For a moment the two parties stared at one another. Garian led a riding of ten of his father's personal guard, all neat in their blue livery, all well armed and military in their formation. In addition, there were six or seven noble youths from Court, equally well armed. Connor was very aware of how his own group appeared—mostly young prentices, wearing ill-fitted borrowed clothing, everyone soggy from the rain.

Garian's group had stopped on the bridge. Below ran a fast-rushing stream. There was no way to pass.

Grinning, Garian made a sweeping bow over his horse's withers. "My father sends you his greetings, cousin, and bids me escort you in safety to his camp."

Connor felt sick inside.

Teressa's eyes were dark with anger. "You may return my compliments to His Grace my uncle," she returned in a cool voice. "I will be glad to meet him and confer as soon as I have completed my own plans."

62

Garian's posture must have changed, for he suddenly had to busy himself with a sidling horse. When he looked up, he said in slightly less plangent tones, "You mean, you won't come with us?"

"No," Teressa said.

Dark red edged Garian's thin cheeks, and his mouth opened. Connor could feel his chagrin. But then one of the noble boys snickered, and Garian straightened up, chin jutting. Connor realized two things, the most urgent of which was the fact that Garian was not going to back down in front of all his followers. Panic seized Connor. He could not let the first battle of the war be with people from his own side.

"Let us pass, Cousin," Teressa said.

Before Garian could speak, Connor said quickly, "Here, the weather's going to turn again soon, and we'll all be wet. Come, Garian, Teressa, let's dismount and talk over our plans there under the trees."

Teressa looked at Connor in surprise, but then she nodded and dismounted.

Garian frowned, clearly hesitating, but when Teressa beckoned to him, he made a forceful gesture to his party to keep them in place. Leaping down from his horse, he flung the reins to one of his father's guard and strode toward Connor and Teressa, his gloved hand on the hilt of his sword.

Connor watched him approach, wondering with a kind of desperate hilarity why he hadn't noticed before that Garian was another of Teressa's admirers. He'd seen the truth in that first reaction of dismay—and now Connor tried to figure out a way to warn the angry Princess that Cousin Garian would fight rather than let himself be humiliated in front of all these people, in front of *her*.

But Garian had reached them, and there was no time to talk. He swept an even more elegant bow, and then Connor watched in surprise as Teressa smiled at him and held out her hands.

"Well met, cousin," she said. "You're right to wish to talk first."

Garian opened his mouth, closed it again, then he said hazily, "Talk?"

"About our plans," she responded, clasping his hands. Then she laughed. "Sorry to get those gloves all wet," she added.

"It's nothing," Garian said, with a look of mixed suspicion and confusion at Connor. "Plans?"

Teressa gestured invitingly. "With all your training, you must be here to help us fight Andreus. Am I right?"

"But—well, yes," Garian said, with a short sigh. "That is, my father has a war council made up, and . . ."

". . . and very loyal and quick thinking it is of him," Teressa cut in smoothly, again smiling. "I will rest much better knowing he is also working hard to free Meldrith from the Lirwanis."

Garian tried once more. "He sent me as his emissary," he began in the same self-important tone he'd first used. "I'm to bring—"

Once again Teressa interrupted, this time by grasping Garian's unresisting hand. "And welcome you are, cousin," she said. "We really need people with training and leadership ability to help us."

Garian's thin features flushed. "Leadership?"

Teressa nodded. "My plan is twofold," she said. "I need to build an army. But I also need a trusted group to harass Andreus's forces, to keep them from settling in. Will you help me?"

Garian fingered the hilt of his sword. His bony shoulders hunched under his expensive velvet cloak. He flicked a look at Connor, who on impulse said, "Speak plain, Garian. Whatever you say will not go beyond these trees."

Garian sighed sharply and looked up at Teressa with a strange combination of defiance and sheepishness that at another time would have made Connor laugh. "My father wants me to bring you back, cousin."

"I thought he might," she admitted. "But if I go, you know

64

he'll do his best to force me to have a regent. If it were anyone else, I might not mind, but I don't agree with his policies, and he won't listen to me."

Garian gave a ragged laugh. "He isn't known for listening, is he?"

Hearing years of pent-up frustration under Garian's bravado, Connor felt some of his dislike for Garian dissolving. *It's been terrible enough having Fortian as an uncle. Maybe having him as a father is worse.*

"I have to start now as I'm going to continue," Teressa said. "And I really could use your help."

Garian stared at her a long moment, then he said, "And in return?"

Connor bit back an angry exclamation. All his dislike rekindled, but Teressa's face did not change. She said steadily, "I can't promise much, because I don't have much yet—as you can see. And I won't promise what I don't have."

"But you will, if we win," Garian said narrowly. "What then?"

"You will be part of my governing council if—*when*—we win."

Garian gave a short nod, then added, "And until then?"

Teressa spread her hands. "What is it you want?"

Garian slid another look at Connor, then muttered challengingly, "Commander in chief of your army."

Connor held his temper in rein and waited for Teressa to deny him. But she looked down at the ground for a long time, then up. "All right," she said.

Chapter Nine

*T*eressa watched the expression on her cousin's sharp face change from suspicion to gratification. Then Garian bowed. "I'll tell my people. Now, what's the first plan?" Then he added plaintively, "What are you doing in Rhismoor? My father thought you'd be hiding here, this being the biggest town south of the Haven. Uh, in case those wizards threw you out of the Free Vale . . ."

Teressa schooled herself to look interested as he talked on, but she knew how angry Connor was—one glance at his tense shoulders and his lips pressed into a thin line told her that. She fought the impulse to turn to him, to explain. *But after Garian leaves, ought I to explain?* she thought. *I'm supposed to be in charge. If I start questioning my own orders, everyone else might, too.*

". . . what kind of message should I send to my father?" Garian finished, looking at her expectantly.

"Garian, why don't we ride back to town and find a good place for everyone to stay?" She tried not to sound impatient. "We'll have a war council over some hot supper."

"I can send one of my runners to secure an inn," Garian offered in his self-important tone. "But I don't know how long this region will be safe. The Lirwanis hold everything to the north and east, you know."

Teressa covertly turned her attention to Connor, who still stood silently at her side, his gray eyes dark with emotion.

"Why don't we all go," she said, feeling a little desperate. "Look, it's starting to rain again! I don't want to get any soggier than I am now, if I can help it. We'll talk later."

Garian whirled around and ran back to his waiting troops.

Teressa turned to Connor. Inside, she heard her father's voice, during one of their private talks: *More than anything else, a ruler has to know the art of compromise, how to choose wisely between two difficult alternatives.*

She drew in a deep breath, wondering why her father hadn't warned her how nasty she'd feel after she made the compromise. "I had to," she whispered to Connor. "Don't you see it?"

Connor just inclined his head, almost a bow. A chill settled over Teressa. Without speaking they retraced their steps to the others, and in a few short words Connor told them what had been decided.

Teressa kept her head high and her face calm as Kial turned shocked eyes to her and Laris frowned at the ground. No one said anything as they urged their tired, wet mounts to follow Garian's high-bred horses.

My first crisis as acting Queen. I've made an unwanted ally of a pest and angered my loyal friends. All of a sudden tiredness gripped her, and the soreness she'd fought against all day pulled at her arms and back.

It took all her resolution to keep a calm front as they followed Garian to the town's finest inn. Garian dismounted first and in a loud, lordly voice began giving out orders in Teressa's name. Servants scurried to and fro, some with muted looks of speculation.

But soon their horses were well cared for, and they themselves got rooms, hot baths, and good, hot food. The warmth made Teressa feel the weight of her sleepless nights, and she longed to just fall into the waiting bed with its clean sheets and soft pillows. But she forced herself to put on the one gown she'd packed, now badly wrinkled, and go out.

First, the Head Elder—alone—and then . . .

She reached the hall outside the main parlor and stood at the side of the door, peeking in. Garian and his friends were standing before the fireplace, boasting of the sword tricks they knew.

Teressa backed away one step, two, then turned to the door. Outside, cold air buffeted her face with a wash of stinging rain.

She bent her head and started up the main street toward the town square. Before she had gone a dozen steps, she realized she was being followed. She whirled around, her hand going to the little knife she carried in a hidden pocket.

But then she recognized the tall silhouette. "Connor," she breathed, midway between relief and exasperation.

"You ought not to be going out alone," he said. "There may not be any Lirwani soldiers, but I'll bet there are baddie-peepers nosing about—"

"Baddie-peepers." Hearing Wren's favorite term for Lirwani spies, Teressa felt the knot in her throat grow. She started to laugh, but it came out raggedly. She said, "Oh, I hope Wren is all right!" but she was thinking, *I wish she were here.*

"She'll know how to deal with any baddie-peepers she comes across," Connor promised.

Teressa sighed. "Look—"

"Teressa, I—"

They both spoke at once and stopped.

"Go ahead," Connor said courteously.

"You must see that I had to get Garian on our side," Teressa said. "We can't have our own people fighting, and I won't go back to Uncle Fortian."

"No . . ." Connor looked away, at the buildings around them.

"But?" she prompted.

He just shook his head.

A flash of irritation made her speak more sharply than she meant to. "Well, you can't get mad if Garian is commander in chief. I can't do it without war training. And when I asked you to be my commander, you turned me down."

Connor walked a few steps in silence, then he said, "I turned you down because I know I don't have the experience to direct an army in a battle."

"But Garian thinks he can do it," Teressa said. "Who knows, maybe he's learned something in all those years of fighting lessons he's back there bragging about."

"Teressa, he can't lead an army."

Teressa stopped in the middle of the village square, looking up at the glowing windows of the Council House where just a month ago she had been busy being diplomatic for her father. Again her eyes stung, and she wished, as she knew she would for the rest of her life, that her parents were alive to advise her, to support her.

But they weren't. Instead, here was Connor, who had come to mean almost as much to her. Yet he wasn't advising her. And he certainly wasn't supporting her. She'd met her first crisis as a queen and had made a decision. Obviously he thought it a disaster.

Talking to the Elders is going to be much easier than this, she thought, straightening her shoulders.

She turned a determined smile on Connor and said, "If you're correct, I hope Garian learns fast." She lifted the knocker on the door and let it fall. "Right now I need to get busy finding him an army."

69

Chapter Ten

*W*ren hadn't seen anyone for days, but just the same she scanned the hilly countryside. Nothing.

After leaving the wheelwrights at Hroth Falls, she had seen fewer and fewer people. During the last three days of walking, she hadn't encountered anyone, not even a refugee. She thought that this scarcity of people and the line of mountains to the northeast must mean she had reached Rhiscarlan territory.

Muttering a carefully prepared spell under her breath, Wren slowly raised her hands. From the stream before her several balls of water rose, wobbling comically. But Wren was not in the mood for laughter. This spell was too hard to control.

She held the water balls steady, fighting against a weird sense of weight tugging at her mind. "All right," she whispered. "Let's combine 'em into one big gollop."

The movement spell came next. She said the words, concentrating fiercely on seeing the water balls coalesce, but at that very moment an unseen animal crashed through the nearby shrubbery, breaking her focus.

She tried desperately to regain control, but the balls shivered, then splashed back into the stream.

Plopping down onto the mossy bank, she felt as if she'd been carrying boulders all morning instead of practicing her magic.

"I wish I were better at it." She groaned, getting slowly to her feet. "But I'm not, so I guess I may as well get this over with. And if Hawk turns me into a tree stump, at least my feet won't ache anymore."

She knew that, despite his youth, Hawk Rhiscarlan was a powerful magician, and he had made it very clear during his disastrous visit to Cantirmoor that he was on no one's side but his own. He'd also made it clear that he'd have no hesitation about using magic against someone if he were in the mood. Wren hoped that, though he had the advantage in learning, she had it in imagination. Her magic was not powerful yet, but she was adept at using it in unusual ways, which might serve as some sort of protection.

And she'd know soon. Hawk had recently taken back his family's castle, sending insolent messages to Cantirmoor about reclaiming the family lands. King Verne had not responded only because he saw no sense in ordering soldiers to fight over a sparsely populated area right on Senna Lirwan's border. So Hawk had been left alone—until now. Standing and shrugging into her pack, Wren moved on.

At noon, she topped a hill and saw a shallow valley below her. Across a rushing river stood a fortress set against sheer cliffs. She was surprised. Idres had spoken of a mysterious attack years earlier that had blasted the castle and burned it. Wren had expected crumbling ruins.

What she saw as she trod down the path was that a vigorous rebuilding campaign was going on. And, at least as far as Wren could see, all the work was being done by people her own age or even younger. There was not an adult in sight anywhere.

Several times she got curious looks as she passed work sites, but no one spoke to her. She reached the huge gates, which stood wide open. Feeling her heart thumping inside her embroidered tunic, she marched in. *They don't know I'm a magic student,* she thought, glad now of the anonymous clothes. *To them I'm just another person their age, probably here for the work.*

When she entered the huge flagged courtyard, she saw

71

activity of a different sort. There must have been twenty or more young people busily practicing with swords, quarterstaves, lances, knives. Though no warrior, Wren could see that they were good.

Is Hawk building his own army?

She was just wondering where they'd all come from when a girl her own size waved her sword-fighting partner away, put down her weapon, and approached. She addressed Wren in the Brennic tongue.

Wren knew a few words of it, but not enough to make conversation. She shrugged, but then the girl said in Siradi, "I'm Callay, escaped from a rotten master in the Shipwrights' Guild. Who are you?" Her accent placed her from the area around Hroth Harbor.

Wren said cautiously, "Well, my keepers wanted to make me a potter's prentice, before I left the orphanage."

Callay's brown eyes widened with delight. "Oh, good! We're in need of a potter or two." And then she added, "Go on inside, sign the roster, get a tour, and find a bunk."

"Roster?" Wren repeated.

Callay nodded. "Sure. Our only rule is, you work for your food. Roster's so they know how many the kitchen crew is cooking for." She added proudly, "Other than that, we don't have any rules."

"None?" Wren said doubtfully. "What if there's a disagreement?"

Callay shrugged, pointing at the weapons. "Fight your own battles."

"Thanks," Wren said, and Callay promptly returned to her practice.

No rules? A surge of longing swept through Wren. *What freedom!*

As she walked toward the keep, Wren glanced back, saw Callay working energetically with her sword again. Wren thought about the way Callay had said "rotten master," with such proud defiance. It reminded her of the way Garian Rhis-

72

mordith and his friends gave their titles—like waving a banner. What was Hawk doing here, making a city for runaways?

Wren walked on, listening to drifts of conversation. She heard Siradi spoken, as well as a couple of southern tongues. And then she neared a group doing some kind of exercise with hoops and balls. A girl shouted something, making the others laugh. Wren recognized the language as Lirwani, which made her feel strange indeed.

Hawk had Lirwanis? *They are either spies—or runaways. After all, if any country deserves running away from, it's Senna Lirwan,* Wren thought. Then she frowned, remembering the terrible spells King Andreus had over his borders to keep people from entering—or leaving. She thought about the determination these boys and girls must have had to brave those mountains and the spells.

"Who's this? Someone new?" A familiar voice interrupted her thoughts.

Wren saw a tall, broad-shouldered boy standing in the wide doorway to the castle keep. She recognized Hawk's dark hair and eyes.

"Come in," he said, and disappeared inside.

This is it, she thought, fighting a strong urge to turn around and run.

Instead she made herself walk slowly toward the door. She entered a huge room, gained a swift impression of stone walls, some of them cracked, with a jumble of furniture in one area. Her attention went to the group gathered around a big table under a hanging lamp of bright glow-globes.

A girl and three boys looked up as Hawk rejoined them. Wren stopped just inside the doorway. "Hi," she said.

"Welcome." The girl, a skinny redhead in a very fancy dress, gave her a friendly smile. "I'm Lorian. Who are you, and how'd you hear about us?"

Wren sighed, sliding her gaze over the boys. Two of them had already returned to whatever they were doing on the table,

73

but Hawk leaned against the table, watching her through narrowed eyes. He smiled faintly.

He's recognized me. And he wants to watch me make a fool of myself. "I'm here as a messenger," she said, gaining courage from her annoyance. "I'm a student from the Cantirmoor School of Magic, and I'm here as Prin—*Queen* Teressa's emissary." She ended on a note of challenge, eyeing Hawk.

Lorian looked surprised, and Hawk said, "Thought I remembered that striped hair. Come in, magic prentice. What was your name?"

Unexpectedly one of the boys spoke up, a weedy fellow with curly blond hair. He seemed familiar. "Wren," he said. "That's Wren."

"Do I know you?" Wren asked, coming closer. She was momentarily distracted by the huge map on the table. It was probably the most detailed map she had ever seen, depicting all the local countries with their rivers, roads, and towns. Mysterious red and blue markings crisscrossed the map.

Wren pulled her attention away and looked more closely at the boy. "You're Alif the stablehand!" she exclaimed. "From the royal palace."

The boy grinned and bowed with mock solemnity.

"And a spy, I gather," Wren added narrowly.

All four of them laughed. "And you aren't?" Hawk retorted.

Wren was fuming by now, but she tried valiantly to hold her temper in check. "No," she said, "I told you I was sent by Tess. Uh, Princess Teressa—soon to be Queen. You know of course that Andreus of Senna Lirwan has attacked Meldrith and killed King Verne and Queen Astren."

"So?" the third boy, a heavyset youth with brown hair and blue eyes, spoke up. His attitude was not friendly in the least. Lorian, standing at the other side of the table, looked on somberly as the boy continued, "So are you here with dire warnings or just dire threats?"

"So, nothing," Wren said, her temper flaring at last. "I can tell this is a waste of time. Good-bye." She turned to march right out again.

"Tell us," Hawk said, walking at a leisurely pace around the table. "You came all this way. Spit it out."

She whirled to face him. "As it happens, Tess is trying to fight against the Lirwanis with a handful of loyal friends. She wanted to know if you'd be interested in an alliance. Go ahead and laugh," she added, frowning at the blue-eyed boy, who snickered meanly. "You can just laugh like a gibbon right up until Andreus marches in here and decides to annex this little city you're rebuilding. Do you really think he won't?"

Hawk bowed, his hand over his heart, and said mockingly, "Attack his obedient ally?"

"You trust him not to?" Wren exclaimed, then gave a big, loud, "HAH!"

Hawk's friends all started to talk, but when Hawk raised his hand slightly, they fell silent. "You knew what I'd probably say, but you came here anyway. That took some courage. And I recall quite distinctly that you and that absentminded Siradi prince evaded my traps with too much success to mark down to mere luck. I'm willing to bet that it was you, and not Connor, who did the thinking on that run. We could use someone with your brains." He added decisively, "Your Teressa is finished. Even if Andreus somehow loses his hold here, Fortian Rhismordith will make sure she never sits on her father's throne. Join us, and make your own rules."

"Join *you?*" Wren repeated. The temptation she'd felt when she spoke with Callay had disappeared at Hawk's dismissive words about Teressa.

"Sure," Alif said. "Peasant, noble, none of that matters here. We're all runaways from some kind of rotten setup. Lorian's a duchess's daughter, at least was until they tried to bully her into marrying some fool whose land happened to be convenient to her family."

"And you, Alif?" Wren said. "What's your excuse? Last I saw, people were treated pretty well at the palace."

75

The boy flushed with anger. "Sure, I was treated well—for a stableboy. But just let me talk about what I really wanted to do, and did they ever sneer!"

"So did they stop you from trying?" Wren countered. "When I finally decided to go for what *I* wanted, no one got in *my* way. Outside of some warrie-beasts, an evil king, and a gryph or two," she amended.

Hawk gave a crack of laughter. Even Lorian turned away to hide a smile, and Wren suddenly wondered if Alif the stableboy represented the other side of King Verne's long-ago wishes. *I wonder if you'd like being a prince any better if you actually had to stand around smiling for hours at court functions and memorize tariff tables,* she thought.

Hawk said, still laughing, "I think you ought to stay here, Wren Magic Prentice. You're wasted on those fools in Cantirmoor."

"Better than the fool I'm looking at," Wren retorted.

"What if we try to change your mind?" Hawk grinned challengingly.

Wren glowered at him, her heart sinking when she realized that his seemingly random strolling around had brought him squarely into her pathway.

She looked quickly about. The way to the door was blocked by Hawk and his blue-eyed friend. She saw the distinctive tile pattern of a Magic Designation in a far corner, partially obscured by some of the jumble of furniture, but she knew she couldn't run fast enough to get there, much less perform the transfer magic, before Hawk or one of his long-legged friends could stop her.

So she glared round at the circle and said, "You can't change my mind. Tess is counting on me to help her, so I need to be on my way."

Hawk snorted. "You're too much fun to waste on a boring princess who'll never get her kingdom back. We'll keep you here."

"No, you won't," Wren said sturdily. "If you're thinking

76

of turning me into a tree stump to keep me rooted, you'd better start your spells right now, because I'm—"

At the edge of her vision the light flickered, and Wren felt the air change, a little like impending lightning, which meant a magic transfer. She whirled around, as did Hawk, to face the Designation.

A tall woman with long black hair appeared. Wren stared at the familiar strong face, the faint smile so much like Hawk's, and gasped, "Idres!"

"Well met, young Wren," Idres Rhiscarlan said calmly, stepping clear of the Designation tiles. She looked around the room, her gaze finally coming to rest on Hawk. "You've grown a bit since we saw one another last, Cousin," she said, strolling forward and glancing down at the map. "What's this? Troop movements of both sides? Almost accurate, too," she added with mock appreciation. "Which side were you thinking of selling out to the other?"

Hawk flushed, reminding Wren suddenly of a much younger boy. "So you've been spying on me, cousin?" He said the final word with a nasty edge.

Idres responded coolly, "Of course I have been. Isn't this my home?" She looked around with an air of appreciation. "I might even want to take it back, once you've finished the repairs."

Hawk made a hasty movement, and Idres said quickly, "Don't even try it, dear boy. You're not strong enough. Not nearly."

"What do you want, Idres?" Hawk demanded.

"I seem to have enough family feeling left to give you a friendly warning," she responded. "You've decided to declare your freedom from any obligations that don't suit your convenience. Teressa Rhisadel will respect that, bound as she is by the notions of honor and loyalty, but do you really think Andreus will if it does not suit *his* convenience?"

"I can take care of myself," Hawk said shortly.

"Can you?" Idres laughed. "Yes, you probably can." She

77

nodded toward Hawk's friends, who stood silently, watching. "But what if he decides to attack them? Will you protect them against Andreus, or aren't they worth the risk?"

Lorian looked up quickly, and both boys turned to Hawk, waiting for an answer.

"We fight our own battles," Hawk retorted. "That's why we're here—complete freedom. That means no more oaths, no more obligations. The weak can't batten off the strong, and the strong can't exploit the weak."

Idres laughed. "The strong will always exploit the weak, my foolish young cousin, unless harnessed by equally strong ties. Never mind. I've done my duty. Whether you heed my words or not is up to you." She walked back to the Designation, then paused. "Though I wouldn't underestimate the Rhisadel girl if I were you. She may not be strong herself, but she inspires loyalty, and if you get enough weaklings bonded together by trust, you'll have an army to reckon with. Good luck . . ."

"Idres, wait!" Wren yelled.

But Idres swiftly made her transfer spell and was gone.

Wren sighed, turning around again. The atmosphere had changed. Hawk looked down at his map as if nothing had happened, but the other three all began talking at once.

Wren was forgotten. She turned and headed straight for the door. No one stopped her—no one seemed to notice.

She had about three steps more until she was free, when once again she felt the weird change in the air that presaged transfer magic.

Looking back, she froze.

Lounging against the wall, a friendly smile on his lips, was King Andreus of Senna Lirwan.

Chapter Eleven

"You've been busy," Andreus said, looking around with an air of appreciation. His gaze fell as if by chance on the map, and he smiled.

Wren sensed danger. Though she certainly didn't feel friendly toward Hawk or the two boys, she couldn't help wishing that Lorian had rolled up that map. It didn't take magic powers to suspect that Andreus would not like his troop movements so carefully recorded.

"Very busy," Andreus added. His round face and large brown eyes looked bland, but Wren heard an edge of irritation in his voice.

"Information's a defense when you don't have much else," Hawk said. "We're rebuilding here, can't defend anything. Yet. So I want to know before any invading armies try to retake my land." Contrasted with Andreus's mild manner, Hawk sounded surly.

Andreus's gaze brushed indifferently past Wren and settled on Hawk's three friends. He murmured something, and Wren felt strong magic pull at her just before a gout of flame erupted from one of the glow-globes and engulfed the map. With a cry, Lorian stumbled back, flames licking at her skirt. One of the boys screamed, bending over his hand.

Hawk grabbed up a water jug and dashed its contents over both victims, then whirled around to face Andreus.

Andreus said, "I am quite capable of protecting my allies."

Meaning Hawk, not the others, Wren thought. How would Hawk answer that?

But Andreus then said, "Where is Idres?"

"She's gone," Hawk muttered, looking back at Lorian, who huddled on the ground. "Arrived, issued some threats, left just before you got here."

Andreus nodded. "Fouling my tracers by multiple transfers—a game I taught her." He lifted a hand lazily to where the map had been. "I can use you in Cantirmoor right now. One of Halfrid's magicians is causing me some annoyance, and I haven't the time to find him. You can do that."

"But I'm busy here," Hawk said.

Andreus's incongruously gentle face just looked sad. Wren held her breath. "Hawk," the Sorcerer-King said, "have you changed your mind about our alliance? I would hate to look on you as an enemy."

"I'm running on my own," Hawk said. "I've enough to do here."

"Either you are my ally or you are my enemy," Andreus said. "Shall I give you some encouragement to make the right choice?"

He lifted his hands, his lips barely moving as he cast a spell.

Wren gazed in horror, the magician part of her wondering how long Andreus had practiced to have spells come so readily and in such perfect control, and the Wren part of her dreading the outcome.

A green glow moved outward from his hands toward Hawk's friends, who were frozen in terror. Hawk started weaving countermagic.

But adept as he was, he was no match for Andreus; Wren could see that right away. Hawk managed to ward the spell, but not very well. The greenish glow splashed away, some of it causing an acrid smell where it touched the stone. Hawk staggered. His effort had seriously drained him.

And the Sorcerer-King was already preparing another spell.

What to do? Wren gnawed her lip. She did not know any of the terrible magic that these two had been studying, but she was certain that her imagination could provide something.

Her gaze fell on a line of raincloaks hanging on a nearby wall. With a quick gesture, she brought the cloaks off their hooks and flung them over Andreus, where they clung like live things.

He cursed in annoyance, trying to fight them off, but the spell kept them clinging. It was an easy spell to counter, though—he'd be free in a moment, and Hawk was still recovering. What to do? Wren looked at the stone ground around the Designation tiles. Surely there had to be rock underneath the castle, as this was a rocky area. If she could just shift the stones, Andreus might lose his balance, giving Hawk more time.

She muttered her moving-spell again, picturing in her mind the stone she was sure existed under the flooring. She felt a hard tug at her mind, the heaviest ever, but fear gave her strength, and she held the heaviness in her concentration while she shaped the last words of the spell.

Then, flinging her hands up, she pronounced the last word: *"Nafat!"*

A tremendous rumble came from beneath the ground. Hawk and the two boys staggered, the one with the burned hand falling, as the Designation tiles cracked and crumbled beneath the mountain of cloaks. Then stone exploded upward in shards, raining the room with bits of rock.

Dizzy from reaction, Wren plopped down onto the ground.

Hawk sprang to the ruined Designation and kicked the cloaks. "Gone."

Alif let out a whoop. "You mean, dead?"

"No," Hawk said. "Disappeared."

"I thought you had a tracer on him," Lorian said weakly, turning a pale face up to Hawk. "So we'd know if he was trying to transfer here?"

"Somehow he found out where I cast it, and dis-spelled it," Hawk said shortly. "Are you all right?"

"My leg." Lorian winced. "It'll be fine if someone has some kerryflower salve. But you know, he'll be back."

"With an army, since he won't be able to get here by magic," the blue-eyed boy added in a faint voice, pointing with his good hand to the spectacular ruin of the Designation.

"I know," Hawk said.

And then, as if reminded by the mess, they all turned to Wren. She fought off the last of her dizziness and got shakily to her feet.

"Seems I owe you one," Hawk said. There was no mistaking the hostility in his tone.

Wren felt like snarling *Don't strain yourself,* but she bit it back. "Do what you want," she said, leaning against the door frame. "My friends don't 'owe' each other, and I don't trade obligations with enemies." She pointed at the Designation. "Sorry I ruined it."

Before any of them could answer, she pushed her way out the door and walked rapidly through the crowd of boys and girls approaching the door from a cautious distance.

Callay ducked past someone and touched Wren's arm. "What was that noise?" she asked, looking frightened. "The ground shook."

"Hawk will explain," Wren said, and moved on.

As she made her way through the big gates toward the road, she thought ruefully that she really was sorry about the ruined Designation, because now she'd have to walk all the way back.

Chapter Twelve

*W*hile Wren trudged back up the trail away from the Rhiscarlan fortress, Tyron sat high in the mountains far to the north. Huddled in his cloak before a little fire, he watched the slowly sinking sun.

In his hands was his scry-stone. He looked from the stone to the horizon, waiting for the sun to disappear. Master Kobel would soon be scrying him from Arakee.

Tyron shifted the stone on his palm, wishing that he had the ability to scry on his own. *Interesting,* he thought wryly, *how despite everything I've learned, I'm always reminded of my weaknesses.*

There had been reminders aplenty these past days. First was the shock of coming to the ruined town, Arakee-by-the-Lake. Despite the burned buildings and trampled, scorched fields, refugees from all along the lakeside had swarmed in, looking for shelter in the ancient caverns that legends held had protected their ancestors hundreds of years before.

The town Elders had been overwhelmed by the sheer numbers and unable to cope with those from outside who did not acknowledge their authority, beyond demands that they *"Do something!"*

As soon as Tyron identified himself, the Elders had turned to him in relief, demanding that he use his magic to unseal the old caves.

Tyron shivered, remembering the sea of waiting faces, the

eyes filled with hope, anger, grief, exhaustion. "What caves?" he'd asked.

Those in the front gasped, and a mutter ran swiftly through the crowd, rising louder than the bitter wind howling outside.

"The Hiding Caves," one of the Elders whispered, his watery eyes anxious. "Those our forebears used in Queen Rhis's rule. Sealed by magic, against a time of great need. That time has come."

Tyron opened his mouth, then closed it again, unwilling to say that he'd thought all those old stories were mere myth.

"Aren't you heir to the King's Magician?" the First Elder demanded.

"I am," Tyron said, "but Halfrid never prepared me for war. We did not know Andreus would attack—" His voice was drowned out by cries of disbelief and anger. And though he tried to explain, neither he nor the Elders were able to control what seemed the beginnings of a riot.

But then Master Kobel walked in, an unlikely figure for a hero—a thin, weedy old man with a straggling beard and bald head, whose fingers were stained with the solvents he used in jewelry making.

He soon made it clear that he was the one who had been entrusted with the secrets to the seals, and furthermore, he knew the way to the caves.

So it was old Kobel, not Tyron, who worked through the night directing the countless families along the pathways into the caverns, telling them where to settle, where to find water, how to organize. Tyron helped, but it was Kobel who knew what to do, and who decided how to do it.

Watching the reddish ball of the sun touch the distant line of mountains, Tyron sighed.

Two seemingly endless days later he and Master Kobel had finally had a chance to talk together. When Tyron tried to apologize for being so ignorant and unprepared, the old man had just laughed.

"I am prepared because this was where I was placed, oh,

84

near to fifty years ago. Before me the magician known as Grandma Mitra spent her seventy years guarding the secret of the Caves. Your Master Halfrid knows about folk such as us, but no one else does, because secrets have a way of getting found out."

Tyron had felt a little better then—but only a little. Now he wondered how many other things he was ignorant of that he should know.

Shutting his eyes, he pressed the crystal against his forehead. "What book did I miss studying that has all the spells we need now?" he muttered.

"None," came an answer, and Tyron almost dropped his scry-stone into the fire. He gripped it hard, and it swirled with color.

"Think of me," came the command.

Tyron recognized Master Kobel's voice, and memory supplied an image. A moment later he saw the magician's round, bald head in the stone. Master Kobel smiled. "You need to watch that," he said. "Your thoughts were out there, clear as day, for any listening sorcerer to catch."

Tyron hunched his shoulders, his face burning. *Another mistake.*

"Don't worry," Kobel went on. "Our good friend Andreus seems to be too busy today to do any listening. Falstan says transfer tracers have been following him all over the map."

"Falstan's alive?" Tyron exclaimed.

"Yes, he is—somewhere outside of Cantirmoor, and he's making things ver-ry nasty for some of Andreus's pet tricksters, for I scorn to call those fools magicians." Kobel's long nose wrinkled for a moment.

Tyron whistled, his eyes on the stone. "Transfers all over? Andreus must be invulnerable. I feel sick for hours if I transfer twice in a day."

"Oh, he might have warded the effects with some enchantment or other, but the price will be that much more terrible," Kobel said, and for a moment his friendly face looked hard and unfamiliar. "And sooner or later that price will have to be paid.

But we had better not be long at this, in case they do get their stones out to spy on us. Laris is waiting—one moment while I link you."

Tyron sat back in silence, trying not to feel guilty about yet another of his shortcomings. Kobel had helped Tyron scry Laris before he set out on his journey, and they had set up this session for sunset on whatever day he was about to reach the border. Tyron knew it would tire the old magician to link two distant scryers together, but Tyron could not reach Laris on his own. And Laris wasn't strong enough yet to carry the link for two.

A moment later he saw Laris in his stone, but he sensed Master Kobel in the background. "Tyron," Laris said. "Where are you?"

"About a day's march short of the border," Tyron replied.

Laris's image froze—it meant she was talking to someone else. Then it spoke again. "The Princess wants to know if you are all right."

Tyron thought about how woefully unprepared he had been for mountain travel in winter, but all he said was, "Oh, I've been a little slow. Has anyone heard from Wren or Connor?"

"Not a peep from Wren," Laris replied. "Kira is with Connor, and we scry each other from time to time. They located two enemy camps and fired both, and they saw some fighting. We lost one of our prenties—little Rissa, one of the new ones." Laris's image in the stone did not change, but her voice took on an edge that Tyron had never heard before. "As for us, Lord Garian is most impatient. Princess Teressa declares we are not yet ready for a major battle, but he wants to get to it."

Tyron shook his head, determined not to let out any of his private thoughts about Garian not being able to lead anything more than a donkey.

Laris went on soberly, "This will be our last scry, for I know I won't be able to penetrate the magic binding Senna Lirwan. The Princess wants you to know that you're always in her thoughts. And in ours as well."

"As are all of you in mine," Tyron said, feeling awkward.

His scry-stone swirled with fog, then went dark, leaving Tyron alone again. He almost dropped his stone, and he looked down, realizing his fingers had gone numb. The sun had set. Carefully he stowed his scry-stone away in his pack, then wrapped himself tightly in his cloak and lay down. *Rissa dead. How many will we be mourning before Halfrid can get back?*

It was a very long time before he finally drifted off to sleep.

He was awake long before dawn, his feet and head aching from the bitter cold. Trying to keep his cloak tight about him, he lit the little pile of wood he'd gathered the night before, and he waited until the lick of flame caught hold of the wood and grew into a small blaze.

He warmed his hands and feet first. Then he pulled out just two of his last six journeycakes and set them near the flame until the faint smell of scorched oats tickled his nose.

He ate them as slowly as he could, for he had only four left. *I'll have to find something to eat somewhere up here,* he thought as he melted some fresh snow in a tiny metal cup. When the water steamed he dropped in three precious tea leaves, then placed the cup carefully on a flat rock while he doused the fire and picked up his pack.

The tea stayed warm for a long time. He walked up the trail with the cup held between his hands, occasionally taking tiny sips.

By the time he drank the last of his tea the sun was high, a distant point of bleak white light. Stopping to put the cup away in his pack, he felt danger prickle the back of his neck. He pulled his cloak over his head and stood still as a statue while a shadow flickered over him.

He did not dare to look, but in his mind's eye he could see all too vividly the huge gryph. He knew its red eyes were spying back and forth as it rode the air currents high overhead. Luckily the spells on the gryphs made their vision poor; his gray cloak would make him appear to be just another rock. Gryphs were ensorceled to notice anything moving, reporting such motion to the distant magician who controlled them.

Only when the gryph was long gone did he dare to move again, stamping to get the feeling back into his feet.

He could sense that the border lay relatively near and he hoped to cross it before nightfall. But late in the afternoon, ugly dark clouds boiled over the snowy peaks from the south, and he was forced to find shelter much earlier than he should have.

The storm howled half the night above the stony overhang he camped under, making sleep impossible. When morning came there were deep drifts of snow obscuring the pathway.

"Unless I'm careful, I'll leave a trail that anyone can follow," he muttered, pulling from his pack the fan of rushes that he'd constructed for just that purpose.

It was tiring work, walking backward to sweep away his own footsteps. His back soon ached and his progress was slow.

It was nearly sunset when he decided he would have to camp. Weariness and hunger were making him lightheaded, and he saw lights and flickering shadows at the edges of his vision.

So he slowed even more, turning blurred eyes to sweep the blue-white slopes around him. A distant peak caught his eye. *Does that one mark the border chasm?*

Yanking down his muffler, he rubbed the back of his mittened hand across his eyebrows. Frost stung his eyes, and he blinked it away. The shadows still flickered. *If those are real, I'm in trouble. If they're not real, I'm still in trouble—*

Then he heard a noise: the distinctive crunch of footsteps on ice.

People? He'd almost forgotten that people existed.

Turning slowly, he wiped his eyes again, then stared in silence at the circle of muffled figures pointing spears at his heart.

Chapter Thirteen

Tyron held out his mittened hands. "I'm unarmed."

"Then you'll live long enough to explain why you're up here," came a harsh voice from one of the faceless figures. "March."

A spear prodded Tyron forward and he scrambled hastily after the leader.

For an endless stretch they zigzagged up the side of one of the mighty cliff faces, then they turned onto another trail cut into the rocky mountainside.

A short descent, then Tyron smelled smoke and—his mouth watered—boiling vegetables. The spear carrier prodded again. Looking down, Tyron saw a narrow trail of stones protruding from the sheer cliff face. The leader of the group walked unconcernedly down this trail, ignoring the measureless drop just beyond.

Tyron followed carefully, noting that what seemed to be rocky promontories in the mountainside were actually houses built right into the cliffs.

They stopped before a low door. One last poke with the spear, and Tyron stumbled into a long room. Blinking, he gained a swift impression of stone flooring, bright scatter rugs, and tall-backed wooden furniture. And, seated or standing in a half-circle, a silent crowd—all facing him. As he sank down onto a nearby bench, he watched with relief as his captors stored their spears along one wall.

Someone said something to him. Then a warm cup was pressed into his mittened hands.

It was some kind of soup, the main flavors being cabbage, carrot, and garlic. Tyron drank it down, welcoming the scalding of tongue and throat.

Alertness flooded back, leaving him painfully aware of his prickling feet and itching nose. He yanked off his mittens and rubbed his face to hurry the thawing, then looked up as a woman put another cup into his hand.

Sipping the tea, he watched several bearded men and a stout, white-haired woman pull up chairs in a circle around him.

"Who are you?" one of the men asked.

"Tyron," he said. "I'm a journeymage."

"Going to Senna Lirwan," the woman asked, "or coming from there?"

"I'm on an errand for Princess Teressa. You know that there's a war on? Begun by the Lirwanis," he added.

The first man gave him a sour look. "We've had one army coming through from that direction, and a couple of parties goin' back, probably lookin' for the first." He jerked his head toward what Tyron suspected was the border. "Both of 'em demanded supplies and ponies."

The third man stroked his beard as he said slowly, "We ain't got enough in store to see *us* through winter, let alone armies. And as for our ponies, ain't been the army yet that returns 'borrowed' animals."

The first man growled, "Way we see it, anyone up here's an enemy."

A murmur of agreement came from behind. The white-haired woman was silent.

Tyron thought dismally of his few journeycakes but said with forced indifference, "Well, I won't ask for anything, and I'll just be on my way."

"Not so fast." The first man glared at him. "Why should we let you go? You'll blab about us to the first scouting party you see."

Tyron stared. "You mean you'd kill me just because I happened to be wandering somewhere near your village?"

" 'Happened to be'?" the man repeated, more surly than ever. "For all we know, you're a Lirwani spy, up here to see what we have."

Before Tyron could speak, the woman said, "When did you eat last?"

Tyron shrugged, trying for offhandedness. "Does it matter?"

The woman turned to look up at the first man. "You needn't murder this boy, Krav," she said with a smile. Despite the white hair, her face had few lines. "Two days, he'll drop dead of hunger."

Krav frowned, switching his gaze from Tyron to the woman. "I know your ways, Olla," he said. "What is your meaning?"

"I merely wish to point out what you are so fond of reminding our youths: to overlook good materials is wasteful, and we can't afford waste."

Krav snorted his disbelief. Behind, Tyron heard a shifting of feet and creaking of chairs. From farther back in the room came whispers—he realized that the room was now full of people.

The old man said, "Think you this magician can help us, then?"

"It's possible," Olla replied. "Why don't we ask him?" She looked about her. "Don't you agree that a few vegetables and a loaf or two are fair trade for safety?"

At that everyone began talking at once. Tyron tried to sort out the words, then a whisper close to his ear turned him around. He found a small boy holding a mug. "Here's more soup."

Tyron gulped the soup down, then sat back, shutting his eyes. Warmth suffused him, restoring a little of his energy.

When he looked up again, the boy was gone.

"Can you make our valley safe from intruders?" It was Olla.

"Seems to me you already are safe," Tyron said. "I never would have found you if you hadn't found me."

She responded quickly, "You were lost. But there are enough who know the proper roads up here. Some of our folk earn their bread serving the traders between the mountain villages, though there's little honest trade left. Can you make us safe from armies and the scavengers who follow them?"

Your life may depend on it. Olla didn't say the words, but Tyron heard them just the same, in the urgency of her voice.

Tyron tried to think. "How many roads in and out?"

"One road, north-south," Olla said, "and two trails. You were on one."

Not what I'd call a trail. Tyron recalled the stones protruding from the cliffside, then turned his thoughts to his magic. After a short time, he nodded. "It might be possible, but—"

Olla did not wait. She rose to her feet and lifted her hands.

Behind her, Tyron heard Krav's harsh, stinging voice: "But we voted—all of us, Ming! As you say, there's a war on, and we have to guard our own. Just because the first straggler we find nosing about is only half-grown doesn't mean he isn't a spy."

"We're not bloodthirsty," a woman called from the back. "It's a matter of safety. We can make his ending more swift and painless than some find out on the trails at this time of year."

"Wait," Olla said, in a voice pitched to carry. "Hold!"

The talking subsided, slowly.

Tyron waited for Olla to speak, but when the room was completely silent, she turned and gestured for him to rise. Tyron did. Olla sat down and looked up at him expectantly. Tyron realized it was now completely up to him.

He scanned the faces before him: perhaps fifty or sixty, all ages, some fearful, some angry.

"I offer you a trade," he said. "For me, a few days' food and safe passage out. And my promise never to return or to talk about the existence of this village to anyone."

"And for us?" a man demanded.

"For you, I think I might be able to make a protective illusion—"

"A Haven!" someone shouted. "Our own Free Vale, that the toffs can't get into."

A cheer went up. Tyron shook his head. "You don't understand—"

"You mean you can't do it?" Krav demanded belligerently.

Tyron looked to Olla, but she just smiled and waited.

He took a deep breath. "Before I tell you what I can and can't do, you need to know that the Free Vale is not just for toffs. Anyone can walk in, as long as they don't have evil intentions toward someone there. They can't disguise those intentions. The ward-magic finds them out. The thing is, the only folk allowed to stay more than a few days are magicians."

Several people whispered behind their hands. Others frowned. Olla looked up at Tyron with a slightly questioning look. *She thinks I'm crazy to be telling them the truth,* he realized. *Does this mean she has a secret?*

Tyron said, "That place is old, much older than Meldrith, and the magic that made it probably goes clear back to Iyon Daiyin times. The inhabitants don't care about local politics any more than you care about their affairs."

More talk, some of it ugly in tone. He raised his voice a little. "The important thing is, the magic that bound that place is lost knowledge. No one can break it—but no one can figure out how to duplicate it completely."

"So you're telling us you can't do your side of the bargain?" Krav interrupted, and behind him someone added sourly, "Some magician he is, eh?"

"Oh, I can," Tyron said. "If I were your enemy, I could make an enchantment to bind this place from *anyone* entering—or leaving—for years and years, but you wouldn't like what it would do to your valley."

People looked less angry than puzzled.

"The magic we harness is what appears naturally in all living things. You can use some and do no harm. But take more, and bind it so that it cannot return to its natural element—this kind of magic is sorcery—and you'll end up with landblight like Senna Lirwan, over the mountains." He waved his hand toward the east. "Or you can have an illusion, which costs very little."

"*Illusion, illusion.*" The word went swiftly round the room.

"But illusions are easily broken—if you know how," Tyron went on. "I say '*if*' because a cleverly made illusion can fool the most powerful mages. You will have to decide if you want one, for it will entail a risk."

Now the room was silent.

"I can cast an illusion over your road and the trails, making it seem that there is nothing but impassable cliff to anyone who comes bearing a weapon. Your traders will see the roads if they don't carry weapons. Scouting parties and armies will just see cliff face, and pass on."

A mutter of approval went up. Krav, though, pursed his lips. "I hear 'there's a catch' in your voice, wizardling."

"There is a catch," Tyron said. "I can't make the spell hold if *you* have weapons. So if you want it to work, you'll have to take all your own weapons and hide them outside the borders of the spell. The first one of you who crosses the spell-border with a weapon will break the illusion."

"What?"

Amid the clamor of voices, Tyron heard two people begin arguing. "Trust our lives to a silly spell?" one gasped.

The other retorted, "And just how long d'you think we'll stand if Andreus sends one of his war parties here, whether we have spears and swords or not, dolt?"

A touch at his elbow brought Tyron's attention around to the boy from before. "Ma says they'll argue half the night. Come with me."

Tyron followed the boy out of the room, hunching his

shoulders against the chilly corridor so far from the fire. They went up some narrow stairs, and then to a small room with its own fire keeping it warm. Tyron saw a bed with a plump comforter turned down and ready.

"We'll have breakfast for you when you waken." The boy closed the door.

Tyron had just enough strength left to kick off his soggy shoes and pull his grubby, wet clothes off, dropping them in a heap before the fire. Then he stretched out on the bed, laid his head on the pillow, and . . .

He woke at last, wishing he could sleep for a week. Remembering Krav and the bloodthirsty villagers, he got up, surprised to find his clothes laid neatly over a stool, clean and dry. His shoes were also dry, and brushed free of mud. In the fireplace, a new fire had removed the chill from the room.

After dressing hastily, he grabbed his pack and combed his hair with his fingers as he went downstairs.

In the dim corridor he found the boy, who seemed to be waiting for him. "This way—my sister has food waiting," the boy said, motioning Tyron into a storeroom off of a huge kitchen. Mouthwatering smells made the emptiness inside Tyron feel as though it started somewhere down around his ankles.

The boy disappeared, and a moment later reappeared, followed by a tall girl Tyron's own age who wore an embroidered skirt and a fringed kerchief that completely covered her hair. Both of them carried trays laden with fresh-cooked food.

"Well," Tyron said when he saw their solemn faces, "is this the last meal for the condemned?" He said it jokingly, but his heart started hammering.

The girl shook her head. "They voted to accept your trade. Krav and the others are now going through the village, collecting the weapons." She smiled a little. "We're to keep you inside until everything is hidden."

"An easy job," Tyron said, stretching his feet out to the fire. "But I'll admit I'm relieved."

"We wouldn't let them kill you," the girl said. "You're safe with us."

"I'm even more relieved," Tyron said. "But you might have told me last night." And when he saw the boy bite his lip, he added, "Why, I never slept a wink for worry."

The boy smiled tentatively.

"I suppose I was snoring when you brought my clothes in," Tyron said ruefully.

"Like thunder," the boy said, grinning. Then he exchanged looks with his sister and, without another word, ran off.

The girl came a step nearer and said, "What magic spells can you teach me?"

Tyron was just shoveling a big bite of crisp, honey-smeared wheatcake into his mouth. When he looked up, the girl was watching him with an intensity that reminded him of Wren, when they first set out to rescue Teressa in what seemed a lifetime ago.

She waited while he took another bite, then he said, "If you want to learn it, you have to go to the Magic School in Cantirmoor." He added with a wince, "Uh, if it's still standing when this mess is over."

"Why can't you just teach me some simple things? I learn fast."

"It's a promise I made," Tyron explained. "We all make it before we pass our first tests. Teaching magic is left to the senior magicians, who can determine whether or not a person ought to be learning it."

"Who decided that?" the girl asked, her eyes steady and dark with some emotion difficult to define.

"I don't know who, but there's a Council of Magicians overseas, which guides schools like ours. That's where my Master is now," Tyron added. "As far as I'm concerned, if more magicians held to those promises, there'd be fewer sorcerers like Andreus running around making trouble."

She seemed about to speak but frowned instead, listening. "They have returned." Without another word, she whisked herself out the door.

Tyron remained where he was, working his way through the excellent food. When he was wondering if he could stuff the last few bites into himself without popping, Olla came in.

"We are ready," she said.

Within a very short time, Tyron was once again outside in the bitter cold, following the villagers through a heavy snowdrift toward the road. When they reached the southern border of the town, Tyron motioned for the villagers to stop. They did. He walked on a few steps.

Speaking softly but distinctly, he performed the spell. The sense of magic built steadily, finishing with the internal heat that indicated the spell had worked and would hold. Then, in perfect silence, the entire cavalcade tromped back through the village to the other end of the road. Once more, Tyron performed his spell.

As they moved to the trail accesses, he caught sight of the girl with the fringed kerchief, and again he thought of Wren. Physically the two girls couldn't have been more unalike— Wren short, round, and sun browned, and this girl tall, slim, and light-skinned. But the girl's watchful observance when he did magic, the way she concentrated on everything he did and said, reminded him very much of Wren.

When Tyron was finished, the village leaders invited him back to the inn for a celebratory meal. On the surface, at least, a party atmosphere prevailed. He sensed that the leaders were waiting for something—and he was proved right when, just before sunset, a youth stamped in, proclaiming joyfully, "It works! It works! I nearly got lost, couldn't see the road I grew up knowin'—and I had to go back uptrail and hide my knife under the rocks before I could find my way in!"

The dinner promptly turned into a real party, with musicians coming in to play merry tunes and, later, more of the villagers turning up, until the room was hot and crowded with dancing and singing folk.

At midnight Tyron slipped away to his room, where he found a fresh fire burning. By its light he repacked his knapsack, making sure his last traveler's journeycakes were still edible. Then he climbed into the bed and slept until a cold hand on his shoulder brought him awake with a start. "Who's there?" he demanded, sitting up in the chilly air.

"*Shh!*" A faint gleam of light from the little window shone on pale hair. "My daughter awaits you below. Dress swiftly, and no candles or witch-lights," Olla whispered.

A short time later Tyron tiptoed down the stairs.

In the bright kitchen, he found Olla at work, making bread dough. The boy and girl were also there. The boy silently handed a small, carefully wrapped bundle to Tyron.

"Food for your journey," the girl said, then set down a tray laden with steaming dishes. "Eat this quickly, for we must depart soon."

"What happened?" Tyron asked, sitting at the table. "Has someone already broken my spell? Are they backing out of the bargain?"

Olla shook her head. "All is well." Then she added, "The early hour is for us, not for you. Orin will take you to your road."

Tyron ate as fast as he could while Olla's daughter, Orin, stood waiting by the door. Within a short time he pulled on his mittens and cloak, and then, having thanked Olla, Tyron set out with his companion in the predawn darkness.

The snowdrifts were very deep, and the wind so chill Tyron felt his nose and ears numbing despite his muffler. He knew he would be numb all over by midday, and he wondered bleakly how he was going to make it over the mountains into Senna Lirwan without falling prey to the deadly storms.

After a long walk, Orin stopped and turned to face him. He could just make her out in the faint starlight peeping through the clouds, her slim form outlined against the softly gleaming snow.

They had stopped on a cliff high above a deep chasm, the village gone from sight. They seemed alone in the world.

"My mother will tell them you used your wizard powers to disappear," Orin said.

"But . . . ?" Tyron prompted.

"But you have a choice before you," she said. "The road to the bridge that spans the border chasm is down that way. You can reach it by nightfall if there are no more storms and you are not seen. Or . . . you can instead be borne by my companion, Fiala. Hist! She comes."

Tyron looked up in the same direction Orin faced. Terror made his heart thunk against his ribs when he recognized the wide wingspread of a mighty gryph wheeling silently against the high clouds.

Tyron dropped to his knees in the snow, but his companion stood fearlessly, her arms upraised. The great bird swooped down, its wings fanning them with great drafts of air and kicked-up snow; then it settled near Orin, its head jerking from side to side as it watched them.

Orin pulled off her kerchief, and Tyron saw long silvery hair fall down her back. "Iyon Daiyin," he whispered.

"One of my foremothers," Orin said, pride ringing in her voice. "Long and long ago—so long we have lost all but her name and the fact that she spoke to birds, as do I, my mother, and my grandmother before me." Orin came close, saying earnestly, "You see why I talked to you of magic. There is little up here but ignorance and prejudice. You *must* teach me."

Tyron shook his head. "I can't."

"Why not?" she retorted. "No one would know. I certainly do not talk of these things to anyone in our village."

"But I would know," Tyron said. He thought about how terrible it must be to have to hide a part of one's nature all one's life, and to remain in ignorance. He shook his head, hating to deny her. "I'm truly sorry."

Orin turned away, looking down toward the village.

"Why can't you go down to Cantirmoor when the trouble ends?" Tyron asked.

The gryph muttered deep in its long throat and ruffled its feathers. Orin touched the bird with a slim hand, whistling softly. The gryph calmed. Orin faced Tyron. "I can't. When I go down-mountain, I feel the magic in me fade."

Like Connor, Tyron thought, amazed. *And yet not completely like.*

"But I will go," she said, lifting her chin, "if you think they can teach me to call upon magic more readily. If they can help me to know what it is I can do, and teach me to do it well. I can't abide not knowing," she added.

Tyron let out a short breath, which clouded, froze, disappeared. "I should warn you that the magic we learn is . . . different from that you've been born with. I know someone who has talents like yours, and he can't seem to learn our magic forms. But we have some information now, and someday I hope we'll have more."

Orin turned her face to the sky for a long moment, then at last looked back. "It is good to know that there are others like me, that my mother and I are not alone, as my grandmother, and my foremothers, thought. I can wait patiently, knowing that," Orin said with a dignity that reached back generations. And then, briskly, "You must go if you are to remain unseen. Climb upon Fiala, and sit securely, for the high skies will be cold and you will go numb after a time."

Tyron looked at the huge bird. "Are you certain she will bear me?"

Orin laughed. "I raised her from the egg. She shares my thoughts, and sometimes my dreams. She will bear you to the gates of Edrann."

Tyron let out a sigh of relief. *I guess I'll make it after all.*

Orin helped him get onto the gryph's back, told him to tuck his legs under the great wingpits. Remembering his chraucan ride the last time he was in these mountains, he listened carefully to her instructions.

Then Orin backed away. The mighty wings lifted and the bird lurched toward the edge of the cliff. First there was a heart-stopping drop, then Fiala spread her wings and soared up, circling around the cliff where Orin stood, a dark speck against the faintly gleaming snow.

With a long, echoing cry, the gryph circled once more and began to beat her wings. Tyron clutched her rough neck, terrified and exhilarated by the wild flight. Up, up the bird flew, into the dark clouds, until all at once she burst free and turned eastward, toward the distant glow of the rising sun.

Chapter Fourteen

Signals?" Connor asked softly.

The ring of faces looked back unblinking. Connor saw twin reflections of his twig flame in each pair of eyes.

"Jay caw for ready, whirler whistle for retreat," Jao whispered.

"And I make a diversion," Kira added. "Some kind of illusion."

"And where do we all withdraw?" Connor prompted.

"Here," everyone said obediently.

"Right. Then let's go."

They separated, Jao, Kira, and Liam to their watch posts in the hillocks surrounding the enemy camp, the rest of the prentices into a defensive line, weapons ready, in case they were needed.

Connor elbowed up to study the enemy camp once more. The brigands slept in a circle around a campfire, their single guard sitting before the flames with a naked sword across his knees, his profile brightly lit. The horses were posted in a line next to a stream just below the camp.

Still lying flat on his rock, Connor heard Palo, the oldest prentice, whisper plaintively, "Why does Connor always get the dangerous job?"

"*Shh,*" came the answer. "Lirwanis might not hear, but the horses will."

Connor soundlessly withdrew. He knew he'd have to talk

to Palo eventually, but what to say? *I do the dangerous job because I have to.* It just sounded pompous, he thought ruefully as he moved upstream.

He reached the horses and swiftly quieted them, reflecting that his talent with animals wasn't the entire reason for his taking the dangerous jobs. Nights still brought the haunting memory of their first encounter with the enemy, when little Rissa—who had probably never held a weapon before—panicked and was stabbed in the side by a big Lirwani soldier. Despite what everyone said to the contrary, Connor blamed himself for her death. He could let no one else go forward first into danger.

Working as fast as he could, he cut the rope holding the horses in place, then he cupped his hands around his mouth and gave a jay caw. Moments later a blue light flashed on the other side of camp—Kira's diversion. In the camp, heads popped up, and most of the brigands roused and ran.

Connor leaped onto the back of the foremost horse, clucking to the others. He led them downstream, the direction opposite to Kira's illusion.

The guard who'd been at the fire heard the hoofbeats and turned back, shouting. Connor glanced over his shoulder, saw the man stumble over a rock—he'd blinded himself by staring into the fire. *Something Mistress Thule would have given us a week's worth of nighttime picket duty for,* Connor thought, smiling as the line of horses galloped away.

Connor's gang converged at the meeting place. The bigger ones helped the smaller ones onto the bare backs of the horses, then they rode straight into the stinging rain. Connor was shivering before long, but still he was glad of the nasty weather. Rain would make it much harder for any enemy to follow their trail.

No one complained. They kept riding until Connor heard a welcome noise—the barking of a hound. Others heard just the noise, but Connor heard information in that voice. He shouted, "This way!"

His group obediently urged their mounts to follow as he crossed a swift-running stream, then rode up a rocky hillside. Behind a copse of dripping trees stood a tiny shepherd's hut. Running back and forth before it, tail wagging, was a raggedy dog. Its excited thoughts carried clearly to Connor.

"There's a shed around back," Connor shouted to the others over the rain. "Palo, you and Jao take the horses and see if there's food. They're hungry—those Lirwanis didn't feed them enough."

"Witch-light safe?" Palo asked.

"I think so," Connor said.

The two prentices snapped little lights into being. Palo gave Connor a brief, puzzled look before he went with Jao to carry out the order.

Kial called from inside the hut, "Firewood here! Warmth in a trice."

Connor went in, saw more witch-lights bobbing as the remaining prentices helped to get a fire started.

"How'd you find this place?" Kira asked Connor, pushing her curly black hair out of her face.

He looked at the skinny dog now lying on the hearth. The dog looked back at him, its scraggly, white-tipped tail stirring gently. "I guess we're lucky," Connor said.

Kira whistled, rolling her eyes. "Hope this luck stays longer than the rain does."

A little later, when they were as dry and warm as they could get, and had shared a brief meal, Connor asked Palo, "Would you like to take these horses to Princess Teressa? You'll have to be very careful."

Palo's face brightened—he wanted danger and challenge, that was clear.

"You'll have to take one of the others," Connor said. "Go back to Epin. One of you must wait well in the hills with the mounts while the other goes to the weaver's house. You remember where that is?"

"That village, near the Umeth-waters, where we stayed the second night," Palo said, nodding. "Weaver lived just beyond the mill."

"Talk only to the weaver. No one else. She'll tell you where to find the Princess's camp after you give her this password . . ." Connor went on to detail exactly what Palo—and Jao, who was to ride with him—should do, including what dangers to watch for and how to avoid them.

When Connor was done, the other prentices took Palo and Jao aside, entrusting them with messages for friends in the Princess's group.

Connor sat back and watched, thinking how just a few days had changed them all. Long stretches of running, riding when they could, and going without meals had made them look older, thinner—hardier. Each morning he forced them to practice at arms, and some of them were beginning to show proficiency. Two had even expressed a liking for fighting.

When this is over, what will become of them? Am I ruining them for their chosen studies? Or will they end like Rissa, with no future at all?

Connor sighed. Right now they thought themselves invincible. Lucky. Only Connor knew that it was not his leadership that kept them safe—it was the help he got from all creatures four-footed and winged. But winter was coming on, and food would be scarce. Animals would also become scarce, running westward to the warmer climate near the Desert. What would happen then, when he had nothing but his own meager skills to rely on?

Chanting interrupted his thoughts. Tired as they were, the prentices had begun their nightly ritual of naming off the Laws and Rules of magic, followed by the long list of Elementals.

When they were done, everyone rolled up in their cloaks except Kira, who had first watch. In the fading firelight Connor looked down at the summons ring on his finger, wishing he had his best friends to talk this out with: Tyron, Wren—and Teressa.

105

Chapter Fifteen

*F*ar to the northeast, Teressa was also awake, sitting in her little tent and writing by the light of a small lamp.

When her pen went dry she warmed her fingers over her lamp, then dipped the pen into the inkwell. Carefully she inscribed the date, and then the results of the morning's negotiations.

> *Promised to Elkin, Mayor of Craeg, free and untaxed foraging for their sheep on the Crown Land south of town, all the way to Griswold Knolls.*

Teressa laid her pen down and flexed her fingers. It was hard to write so small, especially by such dim light, when her entire body seemed to be half-frozen. But her little book was already partially full. She leafed through the remaining pages, wishing that she'd found a bigger empty book at the Haven House. *Well, at least I have this. Now, what else to write?*

She twisted her neck, which was still stiff from the day's long ride, then bent over the book once more. In the ancient Leric script that she had learned once just for fun, she added:

> *Observation: If people think a suggestion comes from someone they respect, they'll obey it. The same suggestion from someone they don't like is sure to cause argument.*

She thought about how Garian had grumped when she had insisted they stay well away from streams, hills, and other "tactically significant" terrain when they first camped. "This is ridiculous," Garian had said. "If it rains, this field will get soggy, and it will take forever to hike to a stream to get wash water."

"We'll camp here," Teressa had replied. "I've been told by someone with experience that this is best." She hated to mention Connor, as his name always sparked Garian's temper.

At first Garian scowled, then he asked, "A lesson from the King?"

Teressa opened her mouth to deny it, saw that Garian was—for once—not pestering her with arguments; so she shrugged. "My father taught me a great deal," she said, not quite answering—but it was enough for Garian, who turned away and gave the order for the camp.

Now she put pen, ink, and book away, doused her light, and curled up on her mat. But she couldn't sleep, not until she had reviewed her plans for the next day. *That delegation from Hroth Falls ought to be here. That is, if the message-relay system is still working.*

She tried to calculate how long their supplies might last and where they might get more. *Maybe it's time to sell that ruby necklace I was wearing the night of the attack. If this war drags on much longer, food will become more precious than jewels.*

That was her last thought before sleep overwhelmed her. It seemed only a short time later that she was startled awake again by the crunch of footsteps outside her tent.

"Highness." The whisper somehow managed to sound apologetic.

Teressa lifted her head. Cold air shocked her into sitting up quickly. Her braid caught under her elbow, jerking her head painfully back. She bit her lip against a scream of annoyance and scrabbled in the dark for the few hairpins she had left. Winding her scruffy braid tightly around her head twice, she jabbed the pins in to hold it. It been more than a week since she had been able to wash her hair, and at least four days since she'd had the time to unplait and comb it.

107

She pulled her heaviest tunic over her head, jammed her feet into her boots, and thrust her knife down the top of one.

"I'm ready," she murmured, pulling on her gloves as she stepped out of the tent.

Omric Balaran of Croem waited, holding two blunted swords. "You still wish to do this, Highness?" Omric asked respectfully. "I—well, I saw a light in your tent very late."

"Practice every day, Omric," Teressa said. "It's not the will I'm lacking, it's the hairpins."

Omric chuckled. His long form was barely visible in the weak predawn light as they walked away from the camp. They headed for a copse of trees, an uneven outline against the deep blue sky.

"Stop!" a voice challenged on their right. "Who's there?"

"Omric and Teressa." She was pleased that the unseen sentry was alert. *Place them in a circle outside the camp, a big enough circle that they'll see anyone sneaking up before the sneakers see the camp,* Connor had said.

So far, it had worked.

They found a clearing surrounded by shrubs. As Omric measured off the space, tamping down long grass and kicking rocks out of the way, Teressa took her blade and began swinging it back and forth, thinking of Connor as she did so. Though Omric was a patient and kind teacher, she never missed Connor more than during these morning training sessions.

"Shall we begin, Highness?" Omric suggested.

Connor would have said "On your guard!" she thought.

Clash! Clang! They worked steadily, until Teressa's hands were sweaty in her gloves and her shoulders and legs started to ache. With each session the ache seemed to come a little later, she reflected, and her parries and thrusts seemed to have gathered a bit of strength.

Still, she was breathing hard before Omric even broke a sweat, and then, just as she was trying a difficult maneuver, a hairpin gave, pricking her scalp unmercifully. She staggered back, and one of her braid loops swung down into her eyes. Omric pulled up his blade just in time.

108

"Argh!" Teressa exclaimed, clawing her hair back. She glared down at the churned mud at her feet, knowing she'd never find the missing pin.

"Perhaps we ought to cease for the day, Highness," Omric said politely.

Teressa closed her lips against a heated retort, realizing that they had been at it longer than she'd thought. The weak winter sun had come up behind a thick layer of clouds. Omric's bony face looked anxious.

"All right, Omric," she said, forcing herself to smile, to sound calm. "I'll be along shortly. I think I'll try to find that pin."

He bowed, took her blade, and walked back toward the camp.

Teressa glared down at the mud. The heavy braid loop pulled at the remaining pins, making her itchy scalp hurt even more. With a stifled cry she yanked her hair free, sending the last of the pins flying in all directions. For a moment she stared at the thick, bedraggled braid in her hand. Then a flash of anger made her reach down and pull the knife from her boot. Holding out the braid at arm's length, she sawed wildly until it came off in her hand. At once her head felt lighter, and the remaining hair swirled, free, about her shoulders.

The anger departed as quickly as it had come. She stared down at the long length of hair, now catching little glimmers of auburn light from the strengthening sun. Her mother's hair color.

What would her mother think? How proud the Queen had been of Teressa's long, silky hair, a shining river to her knees. So many evenings Queen Astren had brushed it herself and plaited pearls into it so Teressa would look splendid for some Court gathering.

Tears stung Teressa's eyes. She pressed the braid against her cheek, as if her mother's touch somehow lingered on it.

Distant voices resolved into a sharp cry. "His Grace is trying to find you, Highness," the sentry shouted.

Garian. What is the problem now?

"Coming!" Teressa yelled, hating how shrill her voice sounded.

She stared down at what was now just a length of dirty braided hair in her hand. With all her strength she flung it into the thick undergrowth and watched with grim satisfaction as it disappeared.

Morning baths and a new dress each day are gone, she thought as she started back toward the camp. *Gone are the maids who tied the ribbons on my sleeves and dressed my hair. And gone are the music, the plays, the long conversations about art. Mother, I'm glad you can't see me now.*

Her eyes still stung, but she would not permit tears to fall. As she reached the outskirts of the camp, several people stopped and stared at her. She was intensely conscious of the short hair swinging about her shoulders, just like a boy's.

Garian stood near her tent, and when he saw her, he gaped.

"Garian," she said dryly, "may I borrow one of your hair ties?"

Silently he reached up, pulled off his own, and held it out. She tied her hair back, then sighed. Never mind how many traditions she had just broken. The truth was, it felt wonderful.

"Well," she said briskly, "what is the problem?"

"It's them," Garian said, his thin face reddening as he pointed his handsomely gloved hand toward an angry-looking knot of new recruits. "They won't do what I say." And as a brawny, ragged-dressed boy broke from the group and stalked toward Teressa, Garian added loudly, "If this were the Scarlet Guard, such insolence would earn a well-deserved flogging."

The boy coming toward them flushed with rage. "I'll show you insolence, strutcrow," he snarled, advancing on Garian.

"Hold," Teressa said with all her authority.

The boy made an awkward bow toward Teressa, talking the whole time. "You'll pardon me, Princess, but if I hear any more slunch out of this . . . this tilt-nosed miffler, I'm going to—" He clamped his mittened hand on his sword hilt, breathing hard.

110

" 'Slunch'?" Teressa said, trying to keep from smiling.

"Insults," the boy said through gritted teeth.

"Your name, please?" Teressa asked.

"Rett." His eyes shifted, and he added hastily, "Uh, Princess."

"Never mind that," she said. "What's the problem? You knew when you came that my cousin Lord Garian was to command our army."

"But that was before we found out that he thinks anyone not born with a title is stupid as a rock," Rett retorted. "All we do each day is footle about with dueling practice. Dueling!" He exclaimed with devastating scorn. "They hound us about proper form and gentlemen's rules"—he parodied a stance, left hand on hip and right hand twirling an imaginary blade at a decorously distant opponent—"as if the Lirwanis would *ever* pay attention to that mulch!" His hands formed into purposeful fists. "And then he sets his toady pals over us, when most of them—well, some of them," he corrected himself judiciously, "aren't half as quick as we are."

Teressa pressed her lips together, her mind working furiously. "We need the practice, Rett," she said. "We'll have to work together if we're to be at all effective. This means knowing how to follow the arm signals."

Rett bobbed his head. "I realize that. The signals, even the sword practice, we'll take. But I'd rather be flogged ten times over than follow that clotpole Nyl Alembar, just because he's related to a Rhismordith!"

Teressa's eyes went inadvertently to Garian's clumsy cousin. Nyl was at that moment swaggering about the far end of the practice area, waving a quarterstaff. As everyone watched, he swung it in too wide a circle. One end buried itself in the mud and the other smacked him on the jaw. He yelped and fell with a liquid squelch into the mud.

Teressa saw Rett's lips twitch—he was trying to fight a laugh. His friends on the field roared. Garian sighed.

Glad of her years of practice, Teressa kept her face blank.

111

"Tell you what, Rett," she said. "Form your group into lines and *you* run them through some practice while Lord Garian and I confer."

Rett ran off, shouting enthusiastic orders at his group. Garian shifted impatiently, but Teressa put a hand out, halting him, as she watched the boy briskly chivvy the disorganized mass into two neat lines. Within a brief time he had them all moving through the same sword-fighting warmups that she now used each morning.

"He's good," she said, watching Rett swing his blade until it hummed.

"Lacks training," Garian said, curling his upper lip. "What you see is what I've managed to teach him so far—he'd never held a sword in his life until two weeks ago."

Teressa shook her head. "He's good at command," she said. "I think you ought to make him some kind of captain."

"But he's a peasant," Garian protested in a horrified voice.

Teressa felt a flash of anger so strong she wanted to slap Garian's silly face. She stifled it and stared her cousin straight in the eyes. "Do you really think," she said slowly and evenly, "that the Lirwanis are going to ask for Letters of Royal Grant before they attack?"

"We've been trained at arms for our whole lives," Garian muttered, looking at the ground. "That fool has been trained to mill wheat."

"Rett is right," Teressa said. "You've been trained in dueling, and dancing, and making nasty comments with a smile. We need those volunteers, Garian. We need them more than they need us right now, for we did not protect them, and we really haven't governed all that well. I charge you to find a way to work with him—today. Before the sun sets."

Garian blanched. "I thought I was the commander in chief."

"You are," Teressa said, trying to hide how terrified she was that Garian would run back to his father and betray her.

But if I can't be firm with him now, I'll lose the chance forever. "I don't know how you'll do it—that's up to you. But we have to have an army, cousin. Not two big crowds, which is what they are now."

"Princess Teressa!" A far-off cry caught their attention.

Remember compromise. Teresa made herself smile. "I have faith in you, Cousin Garian." *I want to have faith in you.*

Laris ran up right then, carrying her scrying stone, and panted as she talked. Garian marched away, waving to his followers. Teressa forced herself to concentrate on what the journeymage was saying.

". . . just got the signal. They're on the way."

"On the way," Teressa repeated, then remembered. The delegation from Hroth Falls! She whirled around. "I've got to put on my dress."

Laris nodded. "I just sent a pair of riders to find them."

If I'm fast I might have time to get something to eat, Teressa thought, feeling hunger pangs as she ran back to her tent. She'd skipped far too many meals of late.

In the tent she pulled from a saddlebag the one court dress she had left. Those voluminous sleeves and the long, dragging skirt took up as much space, and weight, as a week's regular clothing plus food.

But it was necessary—she needed everything she could muster to lend her the dignity her new position seemed to demand. There was no throne, no crown, no smiling courtiers or lovely music to surround her with prestige anymore. Just herself.

Her fingers laced the silver underdress rapidly, with the speed those twelve servantless years in the orphanage had given her. Then the blue velvet overdress and its silver belt. She had no mirror, but she knew the gown made her look a little taller, a little older. Her hand hesitated over the rubies. Would they help, or was it foolish to wear jewels in a war camp? *Garian's jewels don't impress anyone but his friends, so mine won't either. I'll leave them.*

113

That decided, she bent to smooth the skirt and her hair swung down to cover her face, startling her. A pang of remorse hit her, but she fought it back as she hunted on the tent floor for Garian's hair tie. *What's done is done. I won't look back.*

Her head was high when she marched out, her skirts bunched in both hands so they would not drag through the mud. More than ever she felt the sheer weight of the gown and how difficult free movement was in it.

At the cook tent, she tore a hunk off the flat panbread that made their main dish, and cut a chunk of cheese from a wheel. Seating herself carefully on a barrel, she ate as she listened for the pounding of horse hooves.

They came very soon. She tucked the bread and cheese under a napkin for later, then walked out to wait for the visitors.

They turned out to be three adults: a sour-looking man and woman, and a man with the smiling blank face of a courtier. This latter had to be the cousin to the baron whose land lay adjacent to the city, which meant the other two were representatives chosen by the most powerful guilds of Hroth Falls.

Teressa conducted them through her little camp, glad that—at least to all appearances—the fighting practice was orderly and businesslike. Those on duty at the cook tent had brewed summer tea from Teressa's precious hoard, and the visitors sat and sipped at it with no change in their expressions.

Their questions were general until one of the guild people turned to her and said stonily, "Why should we risk our people with you, Princess? What guarantee have we, should we win, that you won't turn about and hand off our lands to some fool relative who's already ruined his own lands, just as your father was about to do down south?"

"Now, Runter," the baron's cousin said, smiling in faint reproach, "I'm certain the King had never intended any such thing."

Teressa looked from one to the other, deciding that the smiling cousin was the more dangerous of the two—Runter, though blunt, was honest. "What guarantee do I have that you won't run after every hothead who talks rumor?" she countered.

The woman visitor, silent till then, laughed. "That's for you, Runter," she said. "And you too, Lord Kilyan." Then she leaned forward. "So you want all our able-bodied souls, is that it?"

I've got them, Teressa rejoiced, but again she kept her face smooth. "Not all," she said. "Only a portion, and a small one at that. Your main force—whatever you can muster in secret—ought to stay right at home. Because here's my plan . . ."

Chapter Sixteen

*T*yron laid his hand against the heavy iron-reinforced door high in Andreus's tower and shut his eyes. He felt the ward-spell waiting—not one but two spells.

His heart thumping, he softly whispered his ward-change spell.

". . . *Nafat,*" he finished. Andreus's first ward disintegrated.

Tyron looked about, listening. No sign of roaming sentries on the long stair below. He turned back to the door, his eyes half closed. He could "see" the nature of the second ward—enough like the first to fool someone careless. It was also more lethal.

Swiftly Tyron broke that too, then lifted the door latch and went in, closing the door behind him.

Looking around, he sighed in relief. He had picked the right tower, then—he recognized this room from the time he and Connor were prisoners of Andreus. These were the Sorcerer-King's personal chambers. There would be more traps awaiting him, most likely, but at least he was probably safe from roaming guards. Somehow Tyron knew that Andreus would not like his minions making free with his private rooms in his absence.

Tyron stood on a plush rug of deep blue and scanned the room more carefully. The carved furniture, the hanging tapestries were the same. On a pedestal between two windows stood the great scry-stone, colors winking in mesmerizing patterns deep inside. The stone exuded great evil. Tyron turned his shoulder, fighting off the temptation to look into it.

Instead, he pulled from his pocket a tiny rock, which he flipped ahead. It bounced across the rug and stopped against the far door.

No illusions, then. Hands outstretched to feel the warning buzz of magic, he stepped once, twice, then reached the worn stone beyond the rug.

He felt strong magic guarding the far door before he even neared it. This time it took four ward-breakers before the door was safe. The effort he expended left him feeling drained and sick. Thirst made him dizzy. All the streams around Edrann had been tainted, and he had not been able to get near the municipal wells, which were guarded at all times.

He flexed his hands, then opened the inner door. His bones still ached from the terrible cold high above the clouds. But he was grateful to Orin and her gryph friend. Perhaps he could finish this dreadful task after all.

Then do it.

He drew in a deep breath, smelled a trace of some unpleasant incense, and sneezed as he stepped into the second room. The air was still and dusty. Since he was in the highest tower, he felt it was safe to unlatch a window, just enough to let in some fresh air. Then he looked around.

The room held three bookcases packed with books ranging from ancient-looking and crumbling to newly bound. Behind one of the bookcases was a small Designation. On a worktable sat a worn map with cryptic markings on it in a slanted hand, in a language he did not recognize. Next to the map lay vials and jars of oddments used in magic. Against the far wall was a narrow bed, and next to it a wardrobe of fabulous wood carved by an artist.

Next to that, a huge silver ewer with a silver cup beside it. The ewer was filled with water.

Tyron was only half-aware of his feet moving—suddenly

he was standing over the ewer, his tongue moving dryly in his mouth.

Andreus brings in fresh water by magic, he thought, angered. Outside the city, Andreus's people made do with the bitter runoff from the barren mountains, but their King probably transferred to high peaks in free countries and helped himself to the springs there.

Tyron felt for wards . . . Nothing. The water was safe.

Ignoring the silver cup, he unslung his pack and pulled out his own cup. He dipped it into the water, hesitated, then drank. The water was shockingly cold and tasted slightly flat, as if it had been standing there a time. But it was good.

Feeling immeasurably better, he turned his attention to the books.

A ward-spell protected the bookcase. He removed it. Then, one by one, he took the books down and leafed through them. Mostly histories, some in languages he did not know. He worked until the last of the daylight faded. Then he created the tiniest witch-light, barely enough to see by, lest the light glow in the windows and alert the sentries on the walls below.

Where were the magic books?

Tired, hungry, Tyron grew impatient. Book after book— until he pulled down one slim one, bound in some kind of pale reptile skin. Looking at the first few pages, he saw with sick horror that the words were written in a clotty darkish brown ink: blood.

Too late, he felt the magic of a ward, and a stone-spell closed around him.

Chapter Seventeen

Wren shut out the snowflakes dancing through the air. The fading light. The refugees' voices murmuring. The angry rush of the swollen river.

Focusing on the tree trunks standing upright in the water, she held their image in her mind. Then she reached with her thoughts to encompass the bridge of closely interwoven slats now lying on the rocky ground.

She *saw* them move as she murmured the commands for the transport spell . . . and abruptly the voices stopped as the bridge snaked up into the air and stretched across the river, settling gently onto the supports.

Wren released the spell and sat down abruptly on a rock, as drained as if she'd carried all that weight on her own back.

"Can we cross now?" a small boy yelled.

Wren opened her eyes. "No!"

"No," someone else said. "It's trembling." Accusingly, "It's not safe."

"I have to bind them together," Wren said.

Getting to her feet, she summoned all her remaining energy to make the binding-spell. It had to be strong enough to hold the bridge, at least for this season. She had problems making her spells last.

Slowly, drawing magic from the air and water around her, she focused on the bridge and its supports, *seeing* them meld together as one construct. Magic hummed through her, so strong she nearly lost the words.

Despite the new sensation of controlling great power, the words of the spell were familiar. She spoke them without faltering and closed with a triumphant shout: *"Nafat!"* And knew it had held.

"There!" she said, looking at the knot of refugees behind her. "I will go first, to make certain it's safe. But I know it will hold—unless some Lirwani magician comes along and undoes my magic," she amended.

"Then we'll have it to do the hard way," a man said sourly. "As maybe we ought to have in the first place."

"Then the Lirwani soldiers can come and hack it apart," another man said. And to Wren, "Thank you, Mistress."

Wren nodded. Mistress? She wasn't even a journeymage yet, though she'd just successfully performed a journeymage-level spell. But she said nothing, just picked up her pack and walked out onto the bridge, pleased at how sturdily it held.

When she reached the other side, a shout went up. Small children raced across, then back again, as the adults picked up their burdens and made ready to cross. Wren kept walking. The main road diverged after a time, and she took the narrow, northward path.

She knew she shouldn't be doing magic—Tyron had warned against the possibility of Lirwani mages tracing her. But it was impossible not to help when she could. She winced, thinking of the terrible things she'd seen on her long journey: burned villages, destroyed farms, people wandering about looking for safety when nowhere was really safe. And everywhere, food getting scarce, though winter had just begun.

Wren looked up at the gray sky. The sun was setting, the snow beginning in earnest. *It's time to pick a campsite—*

The lightning-strike sensation of transfer magic made her back hastily into a thick fir. *"Yagh!"* she yelled, then blinked in astonishment when Idres Rhiscarlan appeared on the muddy path, her dark gown swirling in the wind. "Idres!"

"You should not," Idres said with a wry smile, "have been doing magic."

"I have to help," Wren protested.

Idres gestured back. "They certainly overwhelmed you with gratitude."

Wren shrugged. "They're angry. Magicians didn't prevent the war, so what good is magic?"

"Verne Rhisadel's army didn't save them either," Idres said.

This was unanswerable, so Wren said, "You traced me through my magic?"

"I did," Idres said. "I've been trying to scry you since you left my cousin so precipitously. Your wards are strong, child."

Wren grinned. Then she had a sudden thought and said, "Tess—"

"As far as I know, your princess friend is alive and flourishing."

"But you won't help her?" Wren countered. Even though Idres was a very powerful mage, Wren was not afraid of her. "You said you wouldn't help King Verne, but he's dead now. Can't you help his daughter?"

Idres smiled grimly. "Andreus is trying to force me to do just that. We will have a confrontation—I promise you that—but it shall be at a place and time of my choosing, not his. As for your friend, she seems to be doing well enough on her own." She gestured to Wren. "And you did well with that bridge," she added. "You will be a fine magician someday."

"Thanks," Wren said, wondering what was coming. Idres had not expended all that magic tracing her just to praise her spellcasting.

Idres said, "Why not start your wanderings early? I can show you where to begin—there is much you could learn in other lands."

"I will," Wren said. "After I help Tess get the country back."

Idres lifted her brows, looking very much like Hawk at his most sardonic. "But that might not be possible."

"Well, then I guess we'll just go on trying until we get old and bent!"

"Or get yourselves killed." Idres laughed softly.

121

"Yes," Wren said, fighting off the chill of fear. "Or killed. So if you're here to try to talk me out of it, I guess we'll both freeze and save Andreus the trouble."

Snow was falling faster now, and the deepening gloom made it hard to see Idres's expression. "I never argue. You must choose to suit yourself."

"I must choose to keep my promises," Wren corrected, annoyed.

Idres lifted a hand, dismissing the subject. "I have been watching my cousin Hawk, as you know. And I have also been watching Andreus's castle. I am very much afraid your friend the magic scholar has been caught in a magic trap."

"Tyron?" Wren squeaked.

"You think you can save him?" Idres asked, her voice mocking.

"Which way is east?" Wren retorted, hiding her sinking spirits. *It'll take weeks to get there,* she thought in despair. *If the Lirwanis or a nasty magic trap don't get me first.*

Idres laughed again. "Ah, Wren! Always to the rescue! Here." She held something out.

Surprised, Wren stuck out her mittened hand and found herself holding a chain with a roundish shape dangling from it. "What's this?"

"A very ancient artifact," Idres said calmly. "And dangerous. Yet I believe you are the one to take charge of it, for now."

Wren could feel powerful magic in it. "What is it for?"

"Shape-changing," Idres said. "You fix in your mind the shape you wish to become and put the chain over your head. Removing it removes the spell."

"Thank you! With this, I can get to Senna Lirwan fast," Wren said doubtfully.

"But?" There was amusement in Idres's voice.

"Well, are you about to hop out with some kind of nasty consequence or price, or whatever, that you forgot to mention before you handed it to me?"

"Do not wear it long," Idres cautioned.

"I remember that lesson well enough," Wren said with a laugh.

"But there is even more danger here," Idres said. "The time I turned you into a dog, I used different magic than that which fashioned the chain you hold. This artifact will transfer your clothing with you, and when you remove the chain you will be dressed as you are now. But it uses magic from *you*—I would not wear it longer than a day. Even that is risky."

"Understood," Wren said. "Why are you giving it to me?"

Idres laughed. "I give it to you because I like you, Wren. I took it from Andreus, who stole it from . . . Ah, that can wait. Restoring it to its owner might make a fine adventure for you when you are ready."

"I've had enough adventures," Wren muttered, but not very loudly.

"As for its cost . . . remember what I told you."

And before Wren could say anything more, Idres quickly did the transfer spell and vanished, leaving Wren alone with her gift.

She eyed the necklace swinging from her fingers. An advantage indeed, though a perilous one. How to use it best?

A flying creature, she thought. What kind? Her first thought was something big, bigger and tougher even than a gryph. *Except in any kind of shape-change spell, making yourself much larger or much smaller than your original shape increases the danger.* She thought hard.

Then grinned. *An owl. A big mountain owl. I can fly all night, sleep during the day in my own shape, then fly again, until I get there.*

She set her pack down at her feet and fixed the image of a large mountain owl in her mind, then lifted the necklace over her head and settled it onto her shoulders.

It weighed more than she had expected, and coldness seemed to radiate from it. The stone in the necklace gleamed a weird yellow. Vertigo smeared Wren's vision. She fell down, dizzy.

123

When the strangeness passed, she found herself very close to the snow, her vision now sharp and clear despite the darkness. The necklace swung from around her neck, a heavy weight, but her clothes were gone, shadow-shapes somewhere at the back of her mind.

She stretched her wings, tried an experimental flap, and bounced forward. Then she gripped her knapsack in one claw and with a *whoosh!* took flight. A cry of delight escaped her in a bone-scraping shriek. She flapped harder, climbed high, and found she was strong and fast.

With another cry, she turned eastward.

Chapter Eighteen

T hey did what?"

The Mayor of Chloo looked up at Teressa, then back at the scrap of paper his messenger had brought him. "They *poisoned* a *whole army?*"

At once the Town Council started talking excitedly, each trying to be heard over his or her neighbor. Teressa rubbed her fingers together, wishing she had her journal at hand. As she listened to the "Prince Connor did what?"s and the "Yes, but did you hear what else he did?"s, she thought, *Never again will I underestimate the power of gossip. It's like a fire in a summer wind—the faster it spreads, the higher it burns.*

She tried unobtrusively to see the paper the Mayor was waving about, wondering from whom he was getting his messages and if they were using a code. She had regular reports of Connor's exploits from Laris, who stayed in scry contact with one of Connor's group.

Listening to the talk, Teressa heard not only embellished versions of Connor's activities—but also reports of daring raids and attacks that she knew he hadn't made.

But she said nothing to correct them. She had seen the cheering effect stories of Connor's exploits had on people. They really enjoyed hearing of someone on their side who was successful against the enemy, even if those successes were only pranks. *He's Doing Something,* she thought.

But now, it appeared, others were also Doing Something—and Connor's group was getting the credit. *Either that*

125

or someone with a lively imagination is making up these stories to boost morale.

"Princess." The urgent whisper cut into her thoughts.

She turned. The master brewer's son, Kalen, motioned to her through the crowd. A cousin to Palo the magic prentice, Kalen was tall, strong, and enthusiastic, but also closed-mouthed. Teressa had asked him to take charge of Chloo's volunteers.

She made her way to him. "What is it?"

Kalen flicked a brief glance around, then said in a low voice, "Lirwanis sighted on the west road. A few soldiers, mostly hired blades. Be here soon."

So it begins at last. Despite her racing heart, she forced herself to sound calm. "Does Lord Garian know?"

"Waiting outside."

She walked straight to the Mayor. "The Lirwanis are here," she said. And as his expression went from surprise to anger, she spoke so that the entire Council could hear. "It's possible they know I'm here, but it's more likely that they just had Chloo next on their attack list. What matters is how we work together to save as much of your town as we can."

"What will they do?" an old man asked, looking grim.

"We've heard they usually send someone in with threats, and then take whatever supplies they need," Teressa answered. "If you give them something, they might not do any further damage."

"They'll want more out of us before winter's over," the Mayor growled. "So what ought we to do, then, sit tight and hand over our extra stores?"

"That might preserve you from worse things," Teressa said. "In the meantime, I will return to my group, and we'll do our best to lead them away from here." She hardened her voice as she added, "The longer this war lasts, the more visits you'll have from them. And each time they'll be nastier. This is why I need *everyone* to respond to my plan. Let us clear Meldrith of the Lirwanis, so when spring comes, we can plant in peace."

The Council members muttered to each other, some look-

126

ing unconvinced. But Teressa saw Kalen nod. They'd follow the plan—he'd see to it.

She whirled about and started for the door. From behind her came the subdued rustle of cloth as the Town Council of Chloo bowed to her back. Despite the sudden news, they had remembered royal protocol. She hoped that that was a good sign.

The wintry air outside smote her face. As she pulled on her gloves, she looked up to check the weather. The stars glittered brightly, as if some vast hand had thrown a scattering of jewels across the sky. She and Wren had once lain on the palace roof counting them, wondering which one was the sun that shone over Eren Beyond-Stars' world . . .

She shook the thought away, saw several people on the run. Foremost was Garian's thin figure, his jeweled hilt catching light from the windows at Teressa's back. *Gleaming jewels—making him a target. I'll have to talk to him about that.*

"They've set fire to that end of town." Garian's voice was strained.

"Fire?" Teressa repeated blankly. "Already?"

A moment later from behind came the Mayor's voice in a wail, "Fire? Fire? They didn't even ask for tribute!"

"We'll ride to attack them." Garian waved his hand at the tall young warriors behind him. From the window light, Teressa recognized their familiar blue tabards—Duke Fortian's retainers.

"Wait," Teressa said, trying desperately to gather her wits.

Garian did not hide his reluctance. *"If* we're going to win," he said between his teeth, "we have to go *now."*

"Of course," she said, her eye on the impassive retainers. She couldn't let Garian ride at the head of a charging band into certain death, but if she criticized his plan in front of his followers, she knew he would stick to it to preserve his prestige.

A part of her screamed impatiently at this delay, but she forced herself to be calm. "Quick consultation, Garian. Private."

Garian sighed and moved around the corner of the building with her. She said, "Do you know how many there are?"

"No, but—"

"Then you could be outnumbered," she cut in. "Look, remember our wedge attack?"

"But that's for the field," Garian protested. "Now, if we surprise—"

"If you surprise them while they're firing buildings, you'll chase each other all over town, and they'll fire the town while they hunt you down," she interrupted again, thinking fast. *Connor said to divide . . .*

"Listen," she said. "One of my father's favorite plans. You send just a couple of our people to lure the Lirwanis. Don't attack them right away. Instead, our people run and let the Lirwanis chase after. Stragglers are irresistible to undisciplined louts like those hirelings who'll attack anyone for money."

"I won't turn my back to that rabble," Garian said proudly.

Teressa buried her hands in her skirt so she wouldn't shake him. "Send our little ones to lure them. Tell them to act scared, and Jao and Palo can make illusory people running as well. Then *you* take your Blues and the rest out to . . ." She thought rapidly. "Yes! That little glen just outside the town." She pointed. "We noted it when we rode in. Form a perimeter so no one can get through. Get Palo to lead the Lirwanis to you, and then you ambush them. Don't let any get away to warn the rest. Then Palo and his group go back for more. Go quickly!"

Garian gave a short nod and disappeared into the darkness.

Above the rooftops, a sinister reddish glow indicated where the enemy were looting and burning. Teressa hesitated. What should she do?

People from the town were running by, some in a panic. Several of the Town Council appeared, carrying torches, and started shouting directions at everyone they could find. Kalen ran past, a sword gripped in one hand, heading toward the red glow.

I'd better watch, she thought as she heard footsteps pounding behind her. She turned, hand on her knife hilt—"Laris!"

"They think . . . you should hide, Princess," Laris gasped.

The town hall lamps were suddenly extinguished, and around them other windows went dark. Laris snapped a tiny witch-light into being and cupped her hand around it so it shone only on the ground.

"I won't hide," Teressa said. "I have to know what happens."

Laris tucked her scry-stone more firmly under her arm and extinguished the light. "Then I'll stay with you," she said, no longer low-voiced. The noise—shouts, screams, crashes—was closer.

Skirting the backs of houses, the two girls peered around each corner before hastening to the next. They stopped at an inn on the edge of a small market square. The houses across the way were all in flames. Red light revealed utter confusion.

How can a commander know what's going on? Teressa thought in despair.

But as she watched, the chaos resolved into two main groups. The attackers, some of whom seemed to be drunk, ran yelling from house to house. There was no discipline in the way they smashed windows and flung things out into the muddy snow. Teressa's jaw ached as she watched a burly man torch a house.

In the square, more of the Lirwani hirelings chased stragglers. A heavy woman, weighted down by a load of valuables, was thrown to the ground in front of the inn. She kicked at her attacker, yelling.

He laughed. "Tell me where the horses are," he roared. "And I might let ye live!"

Horses! In a daze, Teressa realized these must be the same

129

ruffians Connor and his group had robbed. *They tracked their horses to us—they think we're Connor's group! They're firing the town as revenge.*

A moment later high, children's voices added to the noise: "Ooooh! Leave us aloooooone!"

That's Jao, Teressa thought, just as he and two of the others ran across the square, looking back fearfully, their faces pale in the light of the burning houses.

At once most of the enemy in sight dropped what they were doing and took off after them. All but the one trying to subdue the woman, who still struggled mightily.

"Got an idea," Laris muttered, running forward a few steps. Dropping her scry-stone in the snow, she wove signs in the air. The ruffian jerked up when he saw five big soldiers in the livery of the King's Scarlet Guard step menacingly from the shadows on the inn porch.

He didn't stay to see if they were real. As soon as he was gone, Laris went to help the woman get up, and Teressa ran into the square—in time to see her forces racing purposefully after the enemy.

It's working, it's working, she thought, exulting. From the inn came the smell of baking cinnamon buns. *Someone better take those out now—they're done,* she thought, remembering her kitchen-duty days at Three Groves Orphanage.

The thought of those buns made her want to laugh, but she knew that as a danger sign. The dark lumps in the snow that no longer moved, the burning houses, the fact that her presence had caused this attack on the unsuspecting town, all of this brought the hated ache to her throat.

Tears are useless. She gritted her teeth and balled her fists. *And Chloo would have been attacked anyway.*

Laris came back to Teressa's side. "They all ran off that way."

"Let's go," Teressa said. "I know where they are."

Laris picked up her scry-stone and tucked it under her arm.

Distant shouts echoed as the girls slogged through the

130

mud toward a rise just outside the town. From this vantage Teressa gazed out over the area illuminated by burning houses and barns.

She saw people running back and forth crazily, their shouts faint on the wintry breeze. Wisps of acrid smoke stung her eyes, but she ignored it, concentrating on making sense of the confusion below.

And presently she did. She watched several small figures emerge from a side road into the town, chased by a pack of Lirwanis. They scattered on a faintly heard signal, and then— just like the drills—Garian's forces dashed out and attacked the Lirwanis, taking them completely by surprise.

Twice more this happened. Then there was nothing for a longish time.

Finally Laris glanced into her stone's flickering depths. "Palo says the Lirwanis are on the run," she said, her dark eyes wide.

"It worked." Teressa gave a crow of fierce pleasure. "My plan *worked.*"

"I think we took losses," Laris said quickly.

"Let's go."

Teressa led the way back. Despite the confusion that soon surrounded them, Teressa remembered what she had seen, and she found herself giving orders to help extinguish fires, convey wounded, and distribute arms.

Dawn was just lighting the tops of the snowy peaks to the east when they had paid tribute to the last of the dead—two of whom were new recruits.

There was no rest, though, for Teressa's army, tired as they were. They had to get well along on their road to the Forest of Mescath, where Teressa had decided they would hide and prepare for their final attack.

She rode back and forth among her people all morning, trying to give comfort where it was needed, and praise to Garian's followers, and encouragement to those—like Laris— who seemed dazed or grief-stricken.

Teressa tried to partake of everyone's feelings, but

131

privately she kept reliving the memory of her own forces acting in concert, on her orders, while the Lirwanis fell. She gloried in the knowledge that she could make a plan and have it carried through—that she could *win*.

And she looked forward to her next battle.

Chapter Nineteen

With her knapsack clutched in her talons, Wren flew high above the clouds all through the night. The sun was graying the eastern sky when she finally dropped down through the icy fog. Drifting low over the treetops, she watched until she saw a good place to hide, and then landed.

Getting the necklace off had taken some effort the first time, then it got easier. That was the only thing that did get easier.

The necklace made shape-changing very different—and very dangerous. For one thing, resuming human form left her tired and disoriented. Her first night, she had barely had time to wrap up in her cloak before she fell into a nightmare-ridden sleep.

In her owl form the instinct to hunt was very strong. She decided, on her first flight, to make herself wait until she was human before she ate—she sensed that giving in to the owl urges would make her lose her human instincts. By the second day she knew it was the right choice—just because it was so difficult to stick to.

But eating human food helped to clear the owl thoughts from her head. She made herself think about human affairs— and then she remembered her friends. Laris! She ought to scry Laris before she crossed the border into Senna Lirwan and was beyond safe scry contact.

She pulled her scry-stone out of her bag and bent over it. A dark cloud flickered in its depths: danger.

At sundown she tried the scry-stone again, and this time she reached Laris without that sense of something evil waiting.

"Wren!" Laris exclaimed in delight. "Where are you? Are you well?"

"Tell Tess that there's nothing to be counted on from Hawk except a lot of insults. Now I'm off to Senna Lirwan to find Tyron. He's in trouble."

"Senna Lirwan?" Laris looked horrified.

Wren laughed. "I'll be all right. I know my way, and I've got—" She hesitated, then decided it was better not to mention Idres or the necklace. "I've got my magic. How are Teressa and Connor?"

"Teressa is fine. Connor and his group have been a great success! But Andreus is combining his little gangs into big armies, which are too dangerous for Connor to harass. So Teressa called them back to us."

"I'd better go. Say hello to both, and give Tess a hug for me."

Wren put her scry-stone away, ate hastily, then changed form. As she crossed the border that night, the owl instincts were harder to fight than ever before. Near the end of her long flight she got confused and forgot why she was flying in a straight line. Owl instinct fought against her human thoughts, trying to force her to mark out a territory and begin her hunt.

It was a piece of luck (she decided later) that a flying spybird spotted her and decided to give chase. In the terror of outflying the big gryph, she kept her owl self at bay and her purpose foremost in her mind.

And it was lucky, too, that gryphs did not like flying in the clouds. She lost the spybird by diving into the thick gray mass over Senna Lirwan and staying in it for as long as she dared.

When she emerged, there in the distance were the towers of Edrann.

She knew she would not make it to Edrann before daylight, and even if she dared fly into the city, her eyesight would be poor, the daylight too bright for her to see any dangers.

Instead, she used the last of her time to find untainted water, for she remembered how difficult that had been on her last adventure in Andreus's ruined land.

At last she found a stream welling up from underground, deep in a straggly forest far from any human habitations.

She wrestled the necklace off. Human once again, she drank from the stream, then curled up underneath a thick bush and gratefully dropped off to sleep.

When she woke at sunset, she ate an oatcake and some nuts, washing it all down with the cold springwater. As she rolled her cloak up and stashed it in her knapsack, she decided it was time to plan.

How to find Tyron in that huge castle? With her summons ring? But then she'd have to carry it in her claws, and the sentries might see its glow. *I'll circle around once, and if that doesn't work, I'll risk the ring.*

Dropping her knapsack at her feet, Wren flung the necklace over her head. First came the familiar roaring in her ears, then her perspective changed crazily. Her human sense of heat and cold went away, replaced by the owl's sharpened senses of smell, hearing, and vision. She grasped the knapsack strap in her talons and took flight, rising above the trees.

It was fully dark when she reached Edrann. Approaching cautiously, she drifted high above the towers to mark out the sentries, who did not think to look up. She did not want to give them any cause to.

Now to find Tyron.

Riding an eddy in the air currents, she sensed a magic aura around the highest tower. *Either this is where Tyron is, or else Andreus is back, making magic, and Tyron is a prisoner in the dungeon.*

Fear made her heart race. She swooped by quickly and glanced in. Though it was dark inside the tower her owl eyes easily saw Tyron's long body lying on the floor. He looked dead.

She swung around again, trying to fly more slowly. Her

owl self was not made for hovering—the necklace swung dangerously.

Hoo—that window is ajar! Her heart was now hammering. Diving down, Wren flew into the window, which banged against the stone wall, then swung shut just as she hit the floor, wings outspread.

The necklace slid off. Wind seemed to roar through Wren's head, and her body tingled as if stung by a thousand nettles. When the magic cleared she sat up, blinking in the sudden darkness.

Snapping a tiny witch-light into being, she looked around. Tyron lay beside the bookcase, oddly unfamiliar in his dark tunic and trousers. She'd never seen him in anything but a Magic School tunic. He seemed taller than she remembered.

She edged closer, looking down. His face was still and pale. Beside him lay an open book. When Wren reached toward him, the warning buzz of magic made her snatch her hand back. Whatever kind of spell he'd been trapped by was a vicious one.

"Tyron," she said. "Wake up! I'm here."

No answer, of course. She tried a ward-breaker, discovering that whatever kind of spell lay over him was stronger than her magic. After three or four more unsuccessful attempts, she tried to reverse a weight spell and felt something happen, but the magic faded.

It's your turn, she thought at Tyron. *I just hope I can reach you.*

She got out her scry-stone and concentrated on Tyron.

The response was immediate, though Tyron's "voice" was faint. *Wren! Where are you?*

"I'm right here with you," she replied. "You can't hear me?"

I can't hear anything anymore; it's as if I've turned to stone.

"I tried to reverse a weight-spell, but it didn't work. Can you help?"

136

It's a stone-spell. I'll tell you the commands. You'll have to hold the magic in mind while you execute them.

"I'm ready."

Aftas . . .

"*Aftas,*" Wren breathed, calling the shape of stone. Then, one by one, she named the other elements of stone, holding all in her mind until the last command, which freed the object forced into stone. Her head seemed to ring from the gathered magic, and warmth glowed between her hands.

But she held the elements, plus a mental image of Tyron freed. Clapping her hands, she shouted, "*Nafat!*"

And Tyron groaned, moving weakly.

"Thank you, Wren," he whispered, looking up at her through hazy eyes.

She grinned. "I like coming to the rescue," she said briskly. "Now, what can I do to help?"

"Water."

"Where?" Wren spotted the silver ewer. "Oh! Is it all right?"

Tyron gave a faint nod.

Wren saw his cup and filled it, then knelt down beside him.

At first Tyron couldn't hold the cup, so she lifted his head and dribbled the water a few drops at a time between his parched lips. *How am I going to get him out of here?* she thought in despair. *He can't even sit up, much less move.*

But the water revived him to a remarkable degree. He rose up on one elbow and gulped down another cup, then let out a long sigh of relief.

"If it'd been a weight-spell, you might've died of thirst," Wren said.

"The stone-spell guaranteed a live victim for when Andreus did return," Tyron said grimly. "How long've I been here?"

"I don't know, but I've been several days coming," Wren said. "Idres told me about your being here."

"Idres," he said, frowning down at the open book beside him. "Don't touch that thing," he warned.

"Wasn't going to," Wren replied, motioning her witch-light directly over the open pages and squinting down. "Eugh! Either the ink was a nasty kind, or this thing is written in blood!"

"Blood it is," Tyron said.

Wren sniffed in disgust. "I wonder if anyone ever told Andreus that if you run out of ink, you can always use beet juice?"

Tyron laughed. "I don't think this was accidental."

Wren sat back on her heels. "What possible use is making a mess?" She mimed cutting a finger open and using it to write.

"It may not be his blood," Tyron pointed out. "I suspect the value is in the symbolism—that Andreus is willing to go to these lengths in order to master whatever is written in that book."

"Can you read it?"

"This part of the book seems to be in in Djuran, but I only know a few words. The front pages—all I saw before the spell dropped me—are all written in very old Lirwani script."

"*Djuran*." Wren backed away from the book. "It has to be bad, then. I've been hearing scary stories about their Emperor since I was little and used to sneak down to the inn to listen to the travelers' tales."

Tyron nodded slowly. "I think we should destroy it if we can."

"Well, why don't you work on that, and I'll check these others?"

Tyron nodded, drinking more water. "Watch for wards."

"I will," Wren said, making one more tiny witch-light.

Positioning the light to float just above her head, she worked slowly and carefully, checking each book for magic traces before touching it. Then, one after another, she took them down and leafed through them.

Not all were magic books. Histories, books of travels, records. From what little Wren had learned of the language, some

138

of them seemed to be accounts written by past kings of Senna Lirwan.

Some were warded against touching, others weren't. She realized after a time that the magic books—and certain records—were the ones warded, so she stopped looking through any that weren't.

She broke the ward-spells and laid the books aside, then went on. She and Tyron could check the pile together when they were done.

She was on the last shelf when Tyron said, "It won't burn."

Wren turned around. Behind a bookcase so his light couldn't be seen from the window, Tyron had made a tiny fire on the stone flooring, and though he dropped the thin blood-written book right on the flames, the book did not even scorch. He flicked it out, wincing as a lick of flame snapped near his fingers; then, using a tool from the table, he held the book over the fire so the pages hung freely. Even then they did not catch.

"That is not a good sign," Wren said.

Tyron sighed. "If only I could read it!"

"Would you want to use it if you could?"

He shrugged impatiently. "If only there were counter-spells . . . If I could figure counterspells . . ." He looked up, frowning. "Except if this is the kind of magic I think it is—a book of sorcery—then there is no way to fight it without worsening the situation, because it binds magic against itself, *spends* it. Usually to destroy."

"What do we do?" Wren asked.

"I'm afraid that this is what we came for. We'll have to take it with us."

"At least then Andreus can't use it against us," Wren said, touching the book, then pulling her hand back. "There's still magic on it—lots!"

"I know. Probably deadly wards against other sorcerers, like Idres. And maybe other kinds of spells. Yet I believe we must risk it." He indicated the pile of books Wren had made.

139

"First, why don't you go quickly through these others, just in case. I'll try to remove the extra wards and spells from this book. Then let's get away from here before sunrise."

Wren leafed through books, tossing down anything written in a language she did not know. Tyron could look over those when he had finished his spells.

Wren found several narrow books written in a laborious hand that reminded her of her own when she was younger. She puzzled out beginning magic commands and elements, basic spells, all of the things she learned in her first year at the Magic School—except the journals contained none of the Rules and Laws.

This is Andreus's prentice book, she thought, glancing over at the knapsack that held her own. It was strange to think of Andreus being young. *What was he like? Probably thoroughly nasty.*

Laying the book aside, she turned to Tyron.

"That's as much as I can do," he said, rising to his feet. He abruptly sat down again.

"What's wrong?"

"Hunger. At least I have the food I got in the last village. Though I'm afraid it's a bit stale."

Wren said, "Well, I have plenty of food, so we'll be all right."

Tyron opened his knapsack and took out some cheese-stuffed rolls, inspecting one. "Dry, but looks good to me." He took a bite, then looked up at Wren. "So how did you do on your quest?"

"It was a waste of time," Wren said cheerily. "Hawk is a pompous fatwit and a toadbrain, just as we always knew. Now, eat up and get your strength back while I get busy here. Then we can go."

"What are you going to do?" Tyron asked.

Wren rubbed her hands. "I," she said firmly, "am going to make a pie-bed, and then tie all Aguewort Andreus's clothes into knots."

"A what? Is that like short-sheeting? We used to do that!"

"Yes," Wren said. "Just think how fine it will be when Andreus stomps back to this castle after we defeat him, and he climbs into a pie-bed! A nice finishing touch, don't you think?"

Tyron's dry lips stretched into a smile, and suddenly he was laughing.

"Then," Wren went on as she worked at the bed, "he'll open his wardrobe and find the clothes. And as everyone knows, it only takes a moment to tie a knot, but ages to undo it. And I'll bet that none of those books have a spell for undoing knots in clothes," she added in triumph.

"He'll just make the servants untie them," Tyron said, still chuckling.

Wren was relieved to see color coming back into his face. "Oh, no he won't," she said as she worked. "There! That's as good a pie-bed as any I've ever made, and believe me, I made a lot in my orphanage days. Now for the clothes." She turned to the wardrobe.

"Why won't he use his servants?" Tyron seemed genuinely puzzled.

"Because what could be worse for his reputation as a powerful, cruel sorcerer-king?" Wren said. "Have the servants gossiping all over Edrann about those knotted shirts and the bed? Never! He'll sit here for hours, gnashing his teeth and undoing every knot."

Tyron grinned, wolfing down the last of his roll as he glanced at the books Wren had set aside.

"There. *Unh!* That's a good one," Wren said, yanking hard on a shirtsleeve. "I just hope," she said, having a sudden thought that made her pause, "he doesn't *blame* the servants."

"Not with those ward-spells on the doors," Tyron said, getting up slowly. "He'll blame Idres."

Wren laughed as he held up a really splendid velvet tunic of a deep blue with scarlet and gold embroidery. "Hey, this one is nice," he said. "Wouldn't mind having it. Too bad he's so short."

"Probably stolen," Wren exclaimed. "Or else left over from some distant ancestor. Why would a villain want to dress nice? You'd think it would go against the Villains' Guild Compact of Evil."

Tyron waved the tunic. "Villains' Guild?"

"Well, we've guilds for everything else, don't we? Why not for villains? Trade nasty spells and designs for dungeons, swap ideas for sinister speeches . . ."

Tyron shook his head as he knotted the handsome tunic into a mess. "Ridiculous," he said. "I don't believe anyone, even Andreus, wakes up one morning and says, 'Well, good day to start a new career as a villain!' "

"You're saying that there aren't any?" Wren was aghast.

"Not at all." Tyron's slanted eyes looked wicked as he grinned. "But I don't think anyone thinks of himself as a villain. I'll wager Andreus has a dozen excuses for what he does. And even if he did admit to villainy, there wouldn't be a guild, any more than there's a kings' guild. None of them want to risk sharing their ways of getting and holding power."

"Tess won't be like that," Wren said firmly.

Tyron shrugged. His lips parted, then he just shrugged again, a little more sharply.

"Well, she won't," Wren said, and then stopped talking about villains, kings, and power. "There! That's the last of the clothes. Too bad we don't have any rotten eggs to tuck into this pair of boots here, but maybe a few of my withered grapes will do—and this sour apple from your pack."

They shouldered their knapsacks, Tyron's now holding the thin book. "All right," he said, "time to plan how to get out of here. Now, we can use illusions to distract any guards in our way . . ."

142

Chapter Twenty

Cheers rang through the snow-dusted trees as Connor and his group rode into Teressa's camp.

Connor felt his neck getting hot. He was relieved when they halted before a cluster of tents around a huge campfire.

Shouts of welcome, questions, comments, laughter surrounded them as they dismounted. The dog, who refused to stray far from Connor, pranced in and around their legs, barking happily: *Food! Noise! Drink! Fun!*

Connor smiled at the dog, whom he'd named Tip. Then he scanned the jumble of tents. Just as he found the central one a flap lifted and Teressa stepped out into the firelight.

Shock almost made Connor stumble. How could someone have changed so fast?

Her hair. She's cut it, he thought hazily. Maybe that was why her cheeks and chin looked planed instead of rounded, but surely that did not explain the thin line to her mouth, the wariness in her steady regard?

"I'm so glad you're back," she said, holding out both her hands. And in a low voice, "I really need you."

Connor took her hands and gripped them tightly, trying to find words.

Laris appeared from the next tent over, her long face shining with joy. "You're here! You're safe!"

"We made a couple of stops after you scryed us last," he said to Laris, trying to collect his thoughts. And then, to

Teressa, "Liam has the results of the last one—two sacks of apples. We took them off a gang of thieves who were in the midst of a spree. Kial's got a sack of flour, and Kira has the best booty, a big block of butter."

"Skirmish?" Teressa asked.

Connor shrugged. "Very short one. They didn't care much for the look of Kira's reinforcements—totally illusory, of course."

Laris laughed, clapping her hands. "Wonderful! Let's hear the rest of your adventures, or are you hungry?"

"Cold, mostly," Connor said. "Something warm to drink will set me to rights." He paused, sensing a change in the atmosphere. Then he saw Garian Rhismordith.

"Well met, cousin," Garian said politely. He still wore velvet, but it was mud-spattered and stained. "We've been hearing of little else besides your miraculous successes in the field."

Embarrassment burned up Connor's neck. He shrugged.

"Modesty?" Garian's smile was tight. "Please tell us how you're always at the right place at the right time. We certainly could use this gift."

Connor glanced down involuntarily at Tip, who gamboled about with a couple of new dog friends. "Just good luck, I guess," he said.

Garian's smile hardened at the edges. With a graceful gesture, he said, "Well, your good luck is our good fortune." He turned away.

Connor looked at Laris, who said, "Duke Fortian found out where we are, and he's coming to us. We expect them tomorrow."

Shock silenced Connor again. His group reacted with sober looks.

Teressa took Connor's arm. "Which is why I need you. We must talk—we have to have plans ready, plans that he can't poke holes in."

A short time later they all sat down to eat. Ruen's cook team had prepared a good meal (using Kira's butter) but Connor hardly got a chance to taste it. Teressa kept asking him questions about the finer points of battle, until one by one Garian and her other leaders had joined them.

As soon as there was a break, Garian said, "You'll want to hear about the Battle of Chloo, which was *our* first win. See, we entered the town during the afternoon, and this band of Lirwanis must have been trailing your two boys with those extra horses, because . . ."

Connor shifted slightly, trying to hide his impatience. He already knew this story—Laris had told Kira through scry contact. Why did they have to rehash all this old stuff? He turned to Teressa, hoping they could slip away and talk about something else. But she leaned forward, intent.

On his other side, Kira's voice caught his attention. ". . . figured someone should get to taste that soup—it smelled so good. So I dumped out my water and put my flagon into the soup. Then we threw the gallroot in and ran!"

"And no one saw you?" Laris asked, sounding delighted.

"Not us, but they knew we were there, because Connor cut their horses loose and let them go. We rode all night to get away."

Laris hugged her bony knees. "Oh, *how* I wish I could have gone with you. All I do is pass messages day and night."

Kira said earnestly, "Boring as your job was, you are probably our most important person. You hear from us only when we do something, not during all those long boring waits when nothing happens. Huh! I'll probably dream forever of lying on cold rocks watching a camp full of people doing nothing. Or worse, watching them eat when we have empty bellies." She shut her eyes and smacked her lips. "Pepper. Ruen's used pepper in that stew." Opening her eyes again, she got up. "I think I might just stroll to the cooks and see if there are any leftovers."

She got up, and Laris turned Connor's way.

He asked, "Have you heard anything from Wren? Or Tyron?"

145

Laris sat upright. "I haven't told you?"

"Told me what? Hawk hasn't done anything to Wren, has he?" Connor's hand fell to his knife hilt without his realizing.

"It must have happened right after I scryed Kira last," Laris mused. "I can't remember. Anyway, Wren didn't say much about Hawk. But she did say she was off to Senna Lirwan, to rescue Tyron."

An invisible fist of ice squeezed Connor round the heart. "What happened?"

"I don't know, except that Tyron is in trouble, and he must have called to Wren to come help him. She was on her way last I heard. Of course I can't scry them in Senna Lirwan. I don't know enough about getting around the interfering tracers Andreus has waiting."

"Did Teressa know?"

"Not until I got Wren's message," Laris said.

Connor looked across at Teressa, who was now deep in a debate with Garian, Liam, and several others about the best way to lay an ambush. The firelight on her face showed a calm, untroubled profile—an expression he knew now was the one she assumed when she wanted to hide her real feelings.

His attention was caught by a blood red flash as Garian waved a hand. A great ruby ring glittered in the light as Garian gestured again, sharply.

They were all tense. *They're worried about the Duke coming. Not about Tyron and Wren—or why Tyron didn't call us for help.* Connor felt the chill increase. *Why he didn't call* me.

Connor lifted his eyes to the mountains bulking eastward, blocking the stars. His longing to escape from the noise, from the loud talk of killing, was strong. He needed quiet—he needed to think. As always when he felt pulled in several directions, the desire to retreat to the mountains was strong. But this time there was an added urgency he couldn't define.

It was nearly midnight, and both moons were high in the sky, when the campfire began to break up. Teressa leaned toward Connor and whispered, "We'll have some time to ourselves tomorrow." Then she disappeared into her tent, and he found his way to his assigned sleeping place.

The two others in his tent, both nobles he knew slightly from Court, agreeably made room for him, though it was crowded. Connor lay quietly, listening to their conversation. They were at least as tired as he was. Garian had had them drilling most of the day, so they would make a good showing when the Duke arrived.

They soon fell asleep, and Connor tried to follow suit, but there were too many thoughts jangling in his mind: the arrival of Duke Fortian, Garian's jealousy, even the startling changes in Teressa. All were understandable, if not expected. But for Tyron, Connor's best friend for half his life, not to call him when he needed help . . .

Connor lifted his hand out of his bedroll and stared at his fingers in the darkness. He could just barely discern the outline of his summons ring. The stone in it was cold and black.

Was it possible Tyron hadn't been able to contact him? *No—if he could reach Wren all the way from Edrann, he ought to have been able to reach me.*

At last he fell into an uneasy sleep. As he had for so many nights, he dreamed of the Lirwani he had killed. The man wandered in a weird, fog-bound twilight land. Connor tried to call to him in the dream, but the seeking eyes never turned his way, and the man shuffled on.

Then the dream drew him deeper. He heard a kind of echo, the kind that lingers after a great choir has sung a deep chord in an ancient stone hall. As he listened it strengthened, until he heard not human voices, but the harmonics of land and water, of sky and snow and all the life that draws from them, flourishes, and returns to them.

And his dreams changed, until he was soaring high against a cloudless sky, riding warm winds redolent of distant seas . . .

. . . until a ruddy glow burned its way into the dreams, diminishing them with the urgency of its own call. The glow

147

brightened until he blinked his eyes open, to see the stone on his ring gleaming right through his blanket.

He yanked his hand out, thinking joyfully of Tyron. He'd have to waken Kira or Laris to scry for him . . . He rolled soundlessly to his feet, pulled on his boots and cloak.

And found Teressa waiting outside the tent.

As soon as they were out of earshot of the tents, she pointed at her ring and murmured, "It worked! I didn't think it would anymore." She laughed softly. "I've got a surprise for you. Here—this way."

"A surprise?" he asked. "What kind?"

"I won't tell you," she said. "Show you."

"Lead on."

She slipped an arm through his and squeezed it. Then they picked their way over the rough, icy ground. Some of his dark mood from the night before lessened.

"Oh, Connor, I can't tell you how I've missed you," she said.

"And I you."

"How I've needed your experience! And your honesty. Omric is nice, but he defers to me as if I'm made of glass, and you know what Garian's like. Laris is the trustiest of them, but all she knows are her endless magic studies. The smartest is Rett, but he lacks training. And we *all* lack experience!"

"That'll come quickly enough," Connor said, wondering how to shift the conversation away from war. Soon enough the Duke would arrive, and they'd have their fill of court intrigue and war talk then.

"We don't have that kind of time," Teressa said. "I think—I know—we have to strike back fast, or we'll be too weakened. What I've told people is that the entire country will rise on a given day and turn on any Lirwanis at hand. And in every town I've found someone who will make sure they follow through," she added grimly.

"How will they know?"

"We'll use the magicians for communication—and the signal will be an old folk song."

"That's a great idea," Connor said.

"I got it from Wren's favorite play, about Eren Beyond-Stars," Teressa said with a laugh. "Fancy ever getting help for modern problems from ancient history! But that's my grand strategy. I've needed you desperately to talk about tactics for the follow-through."

"I don't know all that much more than you do," Connor said. "Everything I told you I learned from listening to Mistress Thule, and she'll probably be with Uncle Fortian. You ought to talk to her."

Teressa sighed. "Connor, why do you keep doing this? You're really good at fighting, and planning, better than any of the people in my camp who keep pestering me for exalted ranks and powers. Yet last night, whenever people wanted to talk about all your successes the last few weeks, you looked like you were half-asleep. You're good; you ought to be *leading*."

She tightened her grip on him. "Leading and striking for keeps. That story about putting the gallroot in the Lirwanis' food is funny, but if your group was clever enough to sneak into that camp, why didn't you do something useful, like kill the commander? You don't seem to have done any real fighting except in defense—yet you are the one who told me a group is strongest when it strikes first!"

I can't. He was surprised at the strength of this conviction, so strong he thought for a moment he'd spoken out loud.

"Teressa—"

She looked up at him, but there was not enough light to see her face.

He tried again. "Look, even if I wanted Garian's position, you know Uncle Fortian would never listen to me. And why should he? He'll have seasoned troops with him, led by able commanders such as Mistress Thule. Teressa . . ." He stopped and faced her. "I'll tell you what I want to do. I want to go over the border and find Tyron and Wren."

She stopped as well. "What? Why?" Then she started walking again. "We're almost there! See, here's our stream. Just a bit farther."

149

"Doesn't it bother you that Tyron didn't call to us for help? That he called only Wren?"

"She's a magician," Teressa said reasonably.

Connor shook his head. "There's more to it than that—don't you see?"

"Well, what then?" She paused, one gloved hand on her hip. "Are you worried about Wren going into danger? We're *all* in danger."

Connor tried to frame words, but couldn't. Anything he could say would be a trespass into Tyron's privacy, and he no longer had the right to even consider that. "I just feel I ought to go," he said.

"But don't you think that if they need us they'll summon us?" Teressa waggled her ring finger, then gave a little laugh. "Connor, you *worry* too much—and about all the wrong things. Ah! Here we are!"

She stopped and swept an arm around.

Connor looked up. The beauty of the little grotto nearly took his breath away. Slowly he gazed from one end to the other. A cliff of tumbled stones faced him, the rocks a glistening white striated with subtle colorations. Over these a waterfall poured down into a rushing stream. At each side small pools were frozen over into ice. Around the edges, ancient trees grew protectively, their branches etched with a light dusting of pure white snow. A thin layer of fresh snow lay on the ground, like a blanket of softest cotton. Seen in the blue light of pending dawn, this little corner of Meldrith seemed to promise utter peace.

She found this for me, he realized, and turned to her, smiling. *A place of beauty, where we can forget the war—*

She smiled back, but only for a moment. As he reached toward her, she flicked a hand at his cloak, then frowned.

"Connor!" she exclaimed. "You forgot your sword!"

Chapter Twenty-One

Teressa had to laugh at Connor's blank face.

"Did you think I'd forgotten to practice every morning?" she asked. "And here I am, wanting to surprise you with how much I've learned!"

He blinked, half raised a hand. "It's so beautiful here," he said. He looked completely confused. "You really want to churn it all up with fighting practice?"

"Yes," she said, "what else? We're in the middle of a war."

For a moment he looked pained, which surprised Teressa. But then his expression smoothed into polite friendliness. "Right. Well, if you want to practice, then we can."

"But you forgot your sword. By the time we walk back, the camp will be roused, and I'll have to face them all again. They know I'm free until dawn, but after the sun rises, then it's back to work."

"This isn't work?" He pointed to the practice blade at her side.

"No," she said, "it's fun. It's something I can do, can learn, can see progress at." She drew the blade and held it out at arm's length. "I wasn't strong enough to do this two weeks ago, and now I don't even feel it. Maybe in a few more weeks I might be able to defend myself if I'm attacked, and oh, Connor, you've always been big and strong, you just don't understand the feeling of power it gives me." She laughed. "Even better is commanding and winning. I have to tell you about Chloo . . . I know Garian was bragging about his leadership last night, but that was mostly for your benefit. It was I who thought up the plan, and I watched them carry it out, well drilled right to the end."

He was silent for a time, and when he spoke again he surprised her. "Did anyone get hurt?"

"We lost two, and several got wounded. Of course I really feel bad about those two, but—" She stopped. "Connor, you're not going squeamish?"

"Are you beginning to enjoy it?" he countered.

Anger flashed in her. She gritted her teeth against a hot retort.

"Did you want an honest response or not?" he asked.

"Yes," she said, and laughed a little raggedly. "But it's been so long since anyone was honest with me—oh, except for Laris, but she's so gentle. All right then, yes, I do enjoy it. Don't you enjoy fighting and winning?"

"Yes," he said, and tipped his head. "At the time. But not after."

"So you're hinting that I'm beginning to like fighting for the sake of fighting? But it's not true. I look forward to the next battle because I think we can win. And if we win, then we can return to the palaces and gardens and pretty clothes and music and the rest of it, and this time we can enjoy it the more for having earned it."

Connor had turned and was gazing at the sun rays glowing on the mountain peaks. "It looks like a cup of molten gold, doesn't it?" he mused. "About to spill over into the valley."

Teressa glanced up, at first impatient. She felt she was winning a very important argument, though Connor didn't sound angry. She liked the the words she'd just spoken—they would work well in a negotiation.

But though Connor's face was still polite, something in his manner indicated that this was important to him. So she stared up at the mountaintops, trying to see whatever it was that he saw. The rim of the mountain was afire with bright color. As she watched, the sun's edge brimmed, and golden shafts of light splashed down the peaks, vanquishing the last blue shadows of night.

"No one should have to earn that, should they?" Connor went on, as if to himself, so lightly she almost didn't hear him. "Not with bloodshed."

Teressa studied him, trying to read his mood. Silvery sunlight glinted in his eyes and in his dark red-brown hair. A strange feeling gripped her, warmth and coldness at once.

She looked away, back at the mountaintop, trying to marshal her thoughts. The sun was now so strong it made tears sting her eyes.

Can it be true that in mastering the things that interest Andreus I just become more like him? The thought was frightening—and humiliating.

She closed her eyes, savoring the warmth on her eyelids, and made a promise to herself that she would never again let a day end without finding something beautiful in it.

Only then did she turn back to Connor. Pride made her reluctant to concede so quickly, but as she hesitated, the moment was taken from her.

"Teressa," Connor said, taking her hands, "you don't need me, you need a war leader, and you'll have that soon enough. But Tyron and Wren need me. Right now," he added.

But I do need you. Pride wouldn't let her say that—again. She'd said it before, but something had changed.

"All right," she said, glad she sounded calm. "Be well."

He leaned down and pressed a kiss on her forehead. "And you." He turned away and disappeared rapidly among the trees.

Scrubbing a mittened hand across her eyes, she turned back toward camp just as a herald's trumpet pealed. It was a triumphant, alien sound, ringing through the forest. *Uncle Fortian is here.*

She looked back to where Connor had disappeared,

153

irritated with him for abandoning her when she needed him most. *Except he's right,* she thought. *This is my private battle, and if I can't win it, I don't deserve to rule.*

So she entered the camp with her head high and her hand on the hilt of her practice sword. Though she was still wearing her grubby trousers and tunic and patched mittens, she moved as if she were gowned and crowned for a court ball.

"She's here!" Omric called from the edge of camp.

Changes were immediately visible. Her own people were outnumbered by ordered ranks of spear-carrying troops, and liveried servants moved about, silent and skillful, reorganizing the tents. Teressa saw Rett and two or three of his friends standing about watching rather helplessly as Fortian's troops walked around them in a way all the more eloquent for being wordless. The message was clear: The youngsters were not worthy of being noticed.

Teressa wanted to stop and call to Rett, to reassure him, but how? She realized that while she was gone, her camp had been quickly and efficiently taken over. Orderlies were now in the process of setting tents up in neat rows, with a tall blue tent at the center. She spotted twin pennants, one the Rhismordith colors, the other Meldrith's.

A crowd of adults in fine war tunics with gilded swords and long, clean cloaks stood before the blue tent. As Teressa approached, a whisper went through them like a little wind, and they parted, bowing, to make way.

She saw her uncle seated in a fine chair before the blue tent. A great travel carpet had been spread over the churned-up ground, which protected Duke Fortian's glossy boots from any speck of mud.

Teressa stepped onto his carpet with her muddy boots.

Fortian rose. Smiling. A tall, handsome man, he was very imposing in his embroidered battle tunic. "My dear child," he said, stepping toward her. The faint chink of chain mail under his long tunic made him somehow all the more formidable. "I am glad to find you safe, and well." He took her hands, bowed, and kissed her wrists above the worn mittens.

"Welcome, Uncle," Teressa said. Her voice sounded weak to her ears, and she realized that her uncle had pitched his to be heard.

"My son has been telling me of your exploits, my dear," he went on, indicating Garian, who stood stiffly in a small group behind the great chair, his thin face flushed.

Whatever he's told his father hasn't made any difference, Teressa thought. Garian narrowed his eyes in what Teressa realized was a warning glance. She acknowledged it with no more than a slight lift to her chin. Tiresome as he was, Garian had still defied his father in joining her.

Teressa opened her mouth to talk, but her uncle smoothly forestalled her. "I'm pleased to see how well you've endured your hardships." The words were polite enough, but the slight sting in his tone made her suddenly conscious of her grubbiness, which contrasted badly with his royal bearing.

A shifting in the stances of some of the onlookers made her aware that they noticed as well.

She cleared her throat. "Uncle Fortian, I have a plan—"

"How proud your esteemed father would have been," he broke in, silken and smiling, and she realized she had made a grave error.

This is like Court, where the less you give away, the less they can attack. She should have returned compliment for compliment and tried to get him to listen in private.

"And speaking of the King," Fortian went on, making a gesture of respect, which was promptly mirrored by all his liegefolk, "we were able to bring him and the Queen from the palace despite the Lirwani guards. You will be glad to know that we honored them with the death fires."

Reminding me that I was not there—that I ran away. Teressa resolutely kept her face calm, and bowed her thanks.

"Since then we have spent no little time endeavoring to ascertain your safety," he went on in a kindly, reasonable voice that was not a whit less carrying than before. "Thus I will not, I regret to admit, have as much success to report to you as we might have had."

155

Blaming me for whatever he has lost.

"But as for plans, once you have been informed of events of central importance to the kingdom, perhaps you'll want to hear the ideas our best war leaders have been formulating. And in turn, we want to hear what you've observed here on the periphery of the action."

"But I—" She faltered.

"Something you don't understand, dear child?"

I've lost this round; best to retreat, she realized with a bleak flicker of humor. *I'll plan the next attack much better.*

"I was hoping you would join us for breakfast," she said, summoning up her best court smile. "Ruen makes splendid oatcakes."

Her uncle smiled back. "Nothing would give me greater pleasure," he said. "And I shall be happy to wait if you would care to resume the trappings of civilization," he added with a kind laugh. "Helmburi brought some of your gear, and I think you'll find your quarters more comfortable."

He lifted a ringed hand, indicating her own tent, which was now placed at the side a little way from his. Long-faced Helmburi stood patiently before it. His familiar face brought the old grief back without warning.

Her throat constricted, her eyes hot and dry and aching, Teressa gave her uncle as regal a nod as she could manage and walked through the silent courtiers to her tent. On all sides they bowed, but no one spoke a word.

She reached the tent and saw trunks and furnishings within. Inside, a maidservant she recognized from her Aunt Carla's rooms bowed low, her face stony with disapproval.

When Teressa looked back out, she saw two tall women in Rhismordith livery take up station on either side of her tent flap, their spears grounded, their hands on the hilts of their swords. An honor guard.

Teressa sank down onto a silken hassock and buried her face in her hands. Despite all her efforts, Fortian had won. She was a prisoner.

156

Chapter Twenty-Two

*U*nseen on a cliff just above the camp, Connor watched the tableau far below. He saw Teressa standing alone in the circle of Rhismordith troops and courtiers; he saw her bow her head and walk away toward her tent. Though he could hear nothing, he knew from the set of her shoulders that the interview had not gone well.

He doubled a fist and pounded it lightly on a rock. If only he could do something! He felt torn between his desire to be there, to share with her whatever was to happen next, and his instinct to climb upward, to find magic—to find the right answer to all his problems.

He rose to his feet and faced eastward. He remembered the clarity of vision he'd had walking high in the northern mountains with Wren. There, his slumbering Iyon Daiyin heritage had somehow awakened, kindling a latent ability to deal in some mysterious kind of magic that no one knew anything about—except that it was powerful and dangerous.

Maybe if I go high enough, I can figure out how to use it to help Teressa, he thought. *If I go back, Fortian will just pen me up as well.*

This thought bolstered him enough to get him going. He spent the rest of the day toiling upward as quickly as he could, stopping only occasionally, to catch his breath and stuff a little snow into his mouth against thirst.

If I can get access to that magic, maybe I can find food, he thought, scanning the heights. He tried listening within, to see if he felt the magic awakening, but nothing happened.

So he started climbing again, and he kept going even after the sky clouded over and another snowstorm began.

He found a narrow mountain path and followed it upward, hoping it had not been made by warrie-beasts. Occasionally he paused, listening for animals. They would be his only warning if danger were nigh.

When the sun sank beyond the distant line of mountains far in the west, the air turned bitter, and he looked for a place to pass the night. The shadows in the chasms below were creeping upward when he found an old cave, scarcely more than a crawlspace. It smelled strongly of goat.

He curled up in it and tried to sleep.

Again the dreams came, this time more insistent. The wordless music hummed through the images of flight, of impossible peaks and distant skies, making him long to fly until he could find the source and hear its message.

Then the dream vanished. Rocks clattered against stone outside. He struggled to regain the dream, to ignore the sounds, but in vain. He woke. *Noise? Danger!* He peered out of the overhang, just to see a pair of long-legged mountain khevals bound past, their noses twitching.

Sleep was gone. Connor stood up, ignoring the gnawing of hunger. He ate more snow, then began once again to climb.

Fog closed him in for a good part of the day, making sounds and sights eerie. From time to time he stopped, tired and a little dizzy, and listened for the magic, but to no avail.

Maybe Andreus's spells have banished it, he thought in despair, *just as he's poisoned his land.*

Near the end of the day Connor broke free of the fog, but increasing vertigo made him slow. He kept walking, always upward, until the need to rest forced him to stop. He closed his eyes and breathed slowly; and this time he heard the hum, faint and far away. But there.

Opening his eyes, he tried to listen inwardly, to feel the magic about him. A tingle in his fingertips made him blink down at his gloved hands. Was this just a hunger dream?

He laughed, then watched in wonder as his breath froze into a cloud of tiny flakes that drifted, vanished.

And so I will vanish, he thought, feeling a sharp flash of regret. His thoughts turned to his friends: Tyron and Wren. Did they really need him after all? They hadn't called. And Teressa. High above the clouds here, he could acknowledge the disappointment he'd felt when she'd brought him all the way to that grotto—just to practice sword fighting.

The disappointment blossomed into a painful kind of sorrow, something he had never experienced before. *We don't really know each other,* he thought. *We just know the court image. I wanted her to stay the beautiful princess who could recite all my favorite poems by heart.*

It hurt, enough to make him get to his feet again, and he forced himself onward until he staggered and fell against a stone. *I've gone too long without food.*

But all he saw was snow, stone, sky, and a few trees. No food.

He was too tired to go on any longer. So it was time to find a comfortable place to rest; and if it was to be his place forever, then it must be a place of beauty.

Once again he looked about him, and his eye was drawn to a little copse of trees up the trail. He walked slowly upward until he reached them.

Here on a wide cliff was a jumble of ferny shrubs, and towering over them an ancient, gnarled evergreen, its green spines stretching above his head like protective hands.

Connor sank down at the base of this tree and looked out over the distant land. The air was clear, and he could see valley, forest, river. Way in the north, one of the lakes glinted, golden in the westering sun.

He was too high to see anything humanmade. Wars, truces, plans, and plots all faded into nothingness against the mighty land before him. His vision sharpened, clarifying the distant western mountains.

He breathed in and out.

Now his hearing sharpened, and he was again aware of the hum, a harmonic diapason, reaching up through the stones beneath him, through the roots of the tree.

Closing his eyes, Connor listened to the life within the tree, the slow surge of sap, the steady life-giving trickle from light in the spines moving down to the roots.

He felt the tree's monumental patience, and the wordless music intensified until it sang through the stones at his feet and the trunk at his back, and whispered on the cold wind at his face.

His awareness met that of the trees, and then that of the land, and sank, sank, deep within the world itself, and he gave up, gladly, every claim on humanness.

Unknown to him, the day sped by, and then the night, and another day, and another . . .

Chapter Twenty-Three

*T*yron leaned against the cave wall watching Wren, who perched precariously on a pile of rubble. Her scry-stone sat on one knee, magic book on the other. She wrote hastily, glancing from stone to page, then she put her stubby travel pen back in the ink bottle and turned the stone in another direction.

"Here," she called, her voice echoing through the cavern. "Here's another Iyon Daiyin sign!" She held up her scry-stone and leaned back against a stalactite. "It worked again," she exclaimed. "So all you have to do is scry the images of this particular sign, and all this ancient script appears in your stone, as clear as if 'twas painted yesterday. How I wish I could read it!"

"I take it I'm looking at your journeymage project," Tyron said.

Wren nodded happily. Then she paused and made a face. "Oh. You're hinting that we need to get moving. Let me just copy this one last bit—I hope I'm making the letters right!—and then we'll go."

When she had finished, she scrambled down from the pile of stone, sneezing from the dust. "I'm done—for now," Wren said briskly. "Oh, Tyron, how I wish we had the time for me to copy them all now!"

Tyron agreed, feeling a strong sense of relief. As they started up the tunnel, he thought back over their journey from Edrann, wondering if he had done the right thing in letting

Wren use that necklace so much in order to get them to the relative safety of the ancient tunnels bordering Senna Lirwan and Meldrith. The Lirwanis did not seem to have discovered the tunnels yet, probably because they could not sense the magical signs, left by the long-ago visitors from another world, that marked the cave entrances.

From the start, Wren and Tyron had traveled by night, for Senna Lirwan's barren, flat terrain was too hard to move across by day without risking discovery. So Wren had insisted on using her necklace powers to spy out danger, and to locate good water. They'd experimented once and discovered that though Wren could transform to a large animal such as a horse, she tired easily and could not carry Tyron. So she'd used the horse shape to find Lirwani horses for them.

But every time she reverted to her human form, she seemed disoriented a little longer than the last time. Often she'd eat and drop off to sleep without speaking. Once Tyron tried on the necklace when she was asleep, but the magic was too strong, and made him feel wretched.

"That necklace has very old magic on it," he'd said the next morning. And, touching the outline of Andreus's book in his knapsack, he added, "As old as this—and as dangerous. Maybe we should find another way."

Wren just shook her head impatiently. "Idres knows I can handle it, or she wouldn't have given it to me."

So far, she'd been right. During the uncountable days that they'd walked through the caves, when she had not needed to put the necklace on, she'd slowly resumed her happy, curious, talkative self. So Tyron said nothing, but he watched, wondering what hidden background she had that made shape-changing so easy for her, wondering if it would protect her against prolonged use of the necklace's magic.

They reached the end of the tunnel at last. Sleeping one last time in safety, they emerged into an icy morning winter wind. There was the suspension bridge spanning the chasm between Senna Lirwan and Meldrith. Huddling into their cloaks, they started to inch their way across.

The wind made the bridge tremble and sway. Tyron gripped the ancient cables with both hands, shuffling crabwise. The metal was cold, even through his gloves, making his fingers ache.

Twice he risked a look back to check on Wren. The first time he saw her small body clinging to the cable, buffeted by every gust of wind. The second time he looked, it was just in time to see her hands let go of the cable and move something over her head.

The wind drove her against the cable. She stumbled, then ducked under, and as Tyron watched in fascinated horror, she poised on the edge of the bridge, stretched out her arms and jumped. Tyron clung to the rail, unable to look away as Wren's arms lengthened, blurred, then extended in feathered wings. Her flying hair swirled, resolving into gold-and-brown feathers, then a chraucan drifted high over Tyron, the necklace swinging from its neck, the knapsack from its claws.

Tyron drew in his breath, transfixed by wonder. *Maybe I'm wrong,* he thought clinging to the vibrating cable. *Maybe it's just that I don't really trust any magic I don't understand. And I don't understand this.*

When he reached the end of the bridge, he dropped onto the cliff in weak-kneed gratitude. Above, Wren circled once, giving a piercing shriek, and flapped away.

Tyron kicked the snow off of a boulder, sat down with his back to the wind, and pulled some food from his pack. Cold and stale as it was, he forced it down. *At least it's something to do,* he thought dismally, scanning the slate gray sky. A few snowflakes drifted down, promising more.

Then came the welcome sound of a chraucan's shriek. Another shriek echoed off the rocks, from a different direction. As he watched, two chraucans flew down and landed nearby. The one with the necklace hanging on its breast turned its eyes back and forth, clucking at Tyron. He got to his feet, slowly approaching the other bird. It stayed where it was, and he clambered awkwardly onto its back. The bird bounded forward, and then with a stomach-dropping *whoosh*, lifted into the air.

It was a long, arduous air journey in the deadly cold, but Tyron was delighted to see the mountain peaks move by below. Each cliff they passed was one more they would not have to struggle over by foot.

The lower mountains were just in sight when the birds suddenly veered and landed high on a flat peak. Tyron slid numbly onto the snow. "Thank you," he said hoarsely, not knowing whether the chraucan understood or not, or if it even cared. Then he stood up, trying to move his limbs as he looked westward. He could see the southern forests of Meldrith below, but between them and where he stood was at least two days' worth of difficult journey. Why had they stopped here?

He turned, just in time to see Wren's long chraucan neck dip as she shrugged off the necklace. The bird outline blurred and a human shape fell into the snow.

He waited, but Wren did not get up. Stepping near, he bent over and looked down into her pale, drawn face. Icy blue eyes stared straight back at him with no recognition.

"Wren?" Tyron knelt beside her, reaching to touch her.

Wren opened her mouth, but instead of words she uttered a thin, human version of the chraucan's shriek; her fingers curled into claws and struck at his eyes.

Tyron fell backward into the snow, too surprised to speak.

Wren gasped and sat up, looking from one hand to the other in terror—as if they'd changed form, or had taken on a life of their own. She sat there for a long moment, as Tyron got up and brushed the snow from his clothes.

"I'm *really* sorry," Wren said, her voice shaky. "For a moment . . . I was the bird, and I guess they can have bad tempers." Then she said, looking worried, "It's Connor—in trouble, I think. He's somewhere around here."

"Connor?" Tyron repeated, astonished. "Here?"

Wren yanked off her mitten and muttered the spell for the summons ring. Suddenly the stone on her hand glowed bright red. "I did this first thing," Wren explained. "After I left you on the bridge I flew as far west as I could, then stopped and took off the necklace. I did the summons ring spell, hoping it was strong enough to show some kind of direction. Surprised me when I got the light—going this way. So I marked this place, then changed to the bird again, found some chraucans, got one to carry you." She winced. "I guess I stayed a bird too long."

"Maybe it's time to put the necklace away," Tyron said, in relief.

"Here it goes." Wren stuffed it into her knapsack, then looked around, hands on hips. "But still—wings are much more practical than feet at times like this. I just wish we had snowshoes."

"We can make some snowshoes if we can find the right kind of saplings," Tyron said. "That'll speed us a bit. Now for Connor." He spelled his own ring, and turned slowly in a circle. "Up there." He pointed to a peak on which a little growth of trees and shrubs were just visible.

Wren nodded and started clambering up the rocks. Very soon she was crimson-faced and breathing hard, but she toiled grimly beside Tyron. When they were in sight of an evergreen tree, Wren stopped, then gave a sharp cry.

Tyron stared at a jumble of shrubs, tree roots, and snow. Where was Connor?

"Ohhhh nooooo . . ." Wren moaned, and flung herself at the tangle of roots and shrubs, flinging up snow in feverish haste.

A few moments later Tyron saw a vaguely human shape beneath the roots, and he threw himself into helping clear away the tangle. When they finally uncovered Connor's face, it was under a mesh of roots and fir spines. His eyes were closed and his skin as pale as flour. Sticky sap covered his entire body.

"Connor!" Wren yelled. "Can you hear us?" In spite of

the sap and pine needles, she dropped her head against Connor's chest. For a long time she seemed to hear nothing. Unconsciously, Tyron held his breath until Wren lifted her head at last, her eyes huge. "He's alive."

Working together, they soon had Connor freed from the roots. Tyron pulled off Connor's boots and rubbed vigorously at his feet. Wren labored over his hands, kneading them until they were a kind of mottled pink.

At last Connor heaved a great sigh, then stirred and opened his eyes.

Wren and Tyron knelt at his side.

"Connor? *Connor!*" Wren cried. "What happened?"

Connor's gray eyes were clear and aware, and he smiled, just a little. Then he looked over at Tyron and spoke, so low Tyron had to bend to hear him. "Why didn't you call me?"

Tyron blinked. "What?"

Connor swallowed. "Edrann . . ."

Wren gasped. "I know what he means." She said with mock indignation, "So you didn't think I was capable of rescuing Tyron?"

Connor smiled weakly, but Tyron sensed that this did not answer his question. "Connor," he said, "I didn't call *anybody*. I was dropped by a curst stone-spell in Andreus's castle. It was Idres who sent Wren to me."

Connor's eyes closed, and his lips moved, but Tyron couldn't hear him.

"Well," Wren said, looking from Connor to Tyron, "we can talk that over later. Right now, let's get the worst of this sap off him—see, it peels off better than it rubs off. Then we'll find a shelter and have a fire."

By sunset they were settled into a little cave in a rocky palisade, crouched around a merry fire. They melted snow into Tyron's and Wren's cups and put some of Tyron's tea leaves into them, setting them to steep. Then they split up their food, saving the biggest portion for Connor.

He lay beside the fire in Tyron's extra clothes, with Wren's second pair of mittens on his hands, while his own clothes dried on nearby rocks. As they warmed the food over the fire and ate it, Wren and Tyron took turns telling their stories. Tyron watched Connor as they talked. From time to time his eyes went distant, and it seemed he did not hear them. But if they fell silent, he'd blink and say, "What happened next?"

He did pay close attention when Tyron talked about Orin and her background, and he laughed softly when Wren got to Andreus's pie-bed and knotted clothing.

Darkness had fallen, and the wind was sighing around the icy peaks, when Wren said at last, "What happened to you?"

Connor stared into the fire, pausing so long Tyron was afraid he hadn't heard Wren's question. But when she cleared her throat, he looked up.

"I went to look for you," he said.

"With no food?" Wren demanded.

Connor shrugged. "Fortian came to Teressa's camp. I knew if he saw me, he'd make sure I stayed put." He paused, his eyes going distant again.

They waited, silent. It was when Wren reached for her cup to sip her tea that Connor's reverie broke. He said, "I—well, I met a tree. There's no measured time for trees, or not as we measure it. Seemed a short visit to me, but I guess it wasn't." He grinned as looked over at his drying trousers, which still had sap stuck to them. Then his face changed. "I could hear the land."

"Wow," Wren said, leaning forward. "Who—what—how—?"

"I can't tell you that," Connor said. "Not that I wouldn't if I could, but there aren't words for much of what I . . . heard? Felt? None of our human senses quite fit." Once again he dropped into a reverie, but this time he roused himself. "I felt it as music, a melody that always changes and never ends. But there were strained notes here," he said, waving his hand northward. "The land straining against very old binding-spells.

167

The old magic—the Iyon Daiyin magic—is bound, just as the land is, which is why I can't get to it."

Tyron nodded. "We know that some sorcerer long ago in Senna Lirwan's history wove some hefty enchantments over the western border, which is how these mountains twisted into the border curve."

"The chasm was later, wasn't it?" Wren asked.

"That's what Halfrid said. He's still working at translating the few records we have from ancient times. A lot of them were written long after the events, so they read like legend, not truth."

Wren stirred a little impatiently.

Tyron added hastily, "I know that there's sometimes truth in the oldest myths. I found that out at Arakee-by-the-Lake. I'm not surprised that the spells really did change the land—for any look at a map makes that clear—but that there's some . . . awareness, somewhere, that notices it surprises me very much indeed."

"Not me," Wren said. "I mean, every time I learn something new, I also find out that there are at least three connected mysteries I don't know anything about."

Connor smiled.

"But I'm tired," Wren went on. "One thing I learned today is that bird and girl don't mix too well. I think I'll sleep off the bird, and hope I wake up just girl."

"This news about Fortian is worrisome," Tyron said. "Shall we scry Laris?"

"Tomorrow," Wren said. "Tonight I couldn't hold the image. Tomorrow we'll find out if they've moved."

She curled up in her cloak till there was nothing visible but part of a braid. When Wren's breathing had gone slow and even, Tyron said softly, "How did you leave Teressa?"

Connor frowned slightly. Finally he said, "She's excited about her war. And until the Duke tracked her down, she was doing well."

Tyron sifted carefully through those words and decided he

didn't need to ask any more. So he wrapped himself up and lay by the fire. The last thing he was aware of before he dropped off to sleep was Connor's pensive profile, his steady gray eyes reflecting the dancing flames.

What woke him up was the prick of a knife blade at his neck, and Hawk Rhiscarlan's laughter ringing in his ears.

Chapter Twenty-Four

*W*ren woke up with a gasp when hands gripped her shoulders.

Torchlight danced crazily over the wall of the cave. In its light she recognized the boy pinning her down. "Alif!" she exclaimed.

Alif the stableboy grinned, obviously enjoying her shock.

"Arrrgh!" Wren yelled. "Get your hands off me, wormwit!" And without waiting for an answer, she kneed the boy in his side.

"Ow," Alif yowled in protest, letting go. Wren rolled to her hands and knees and launched forward, head-butting him in the stomach. He fell backward into the snow outside the cave.

Scrambling to her feet, Wren looked around wildly—then saw Tyron sitting motionless, Hawk beside him with a knife at his throat. Next to them a girl with dark braids pointed a blade at Connor with one hand and held the torch with the other.

Hawk was laughing so hard Tyron winced when the knife pressed a little too close. "Need some practice, Alif?" Hawk asked.

"I slipped," Alif said grumpily, brushing snow off his clothes.

Ignoring him, Wren sank down onto a boulder. "Well, this is pretty disgusting," she said, glaring at Hawk. "Are we about to meet Andreus, or is this for your own benefit?"

"It's for yours," came the surprising answer. "This"—Hawk lifted his blade a little in a salute, and Tyron rubbed his neck—"is just by way of getting your attention."

"You've got it," Wren said stonily.

Hawk sat back and with an ironic gesture sheathed his knife. The girl also put her blade away, and Alif found his in the snow and sat down, muttering to himself.

"Andreus is on his way to attack your Princess," Hawk said. "What my cousin Idres didn't tell either of us is that she's been protecting the girl from Andreus's magic. But even she couldn't stop that fool Fortian Rhismordith from leading the way right to the Princess's camp."

"How do we know you're speaking the truth?" Wren demanded.

Hawk shrugged. "You don't."

"Supposing you *are* telling the truth," Tyron said. "What do you get out of telling us?"

"Fun."

Alif said in a surly voice, "We don't care if Andreus tromps Fortian, but we don't want to see him get the Princess."

Wren hesitated. Why had Hawk gone to all this trouble? Why didn't he want Andreus to get Teressa? She said in an overly casual voice, "How'd you find us? Tracer spell?"

Hawk nodded. "Your magic yesterday. We tracked you from there."

The girl put in, "Andreus's detachment should reach the Princess's camp in two days—or less."

Tyron looked over at Connor, who said, "Why don't we eat, then go?"

"Eat *as* we go," Hawk said. "If you want to get there in time."

We? Wren did not say it out loud.

While Tyron split their food, Wren tried to scry Laris to warn her, but she sensed danger, and hastily put away her scrystone.

Hawk called out, "Let's move," and led the way. A little

171

farther down the trail, three more of Hawk's group waited, all of them armed and alert. They fell in behind Wren, Connor, and Tyron, sandwiching the three. Noticing, Wren frowned as they continued down the trail. She didn't trust Hawk much past her next breath.

They started out under a heavy layer of clouds. Occasional flurries of snowflakes danced about them, driven by gusts of cold wind. Walking downhill in snow with only a torch to see by was tough enough without the buffeting by wind and weather. Before too long Wren saw that Connor was having trouble walking at all. Breathing hard, he stumbled several times, until Tyron dropped back and, putting an arm under Connor's shoulder, walked with him, taking most of Connor's weight. Wren walked directly in front of them, trying to kick the worst of the snow out of their way.

Hawk set a very fast pace—so fast it seemed a kind of challenge. The others did their best to keep up. Wren was determined not to earn his derision by complaining. *Unless on Connor's behalf,* she thought, looking back just as Connor stumbled again.

The crunch of ice and the sudden blue glow of a tiny witch-light brought Wren's attention forward again. Hawk walked beside her. "What's wrong with the Siradi prince?" he asked, jerking his chin toward Connor. "He used to being carried?"

Wren ignored the sarcasm. "You'd have trouble too if you'd spent a couple of weeks frozen beneath a tree."

Hawk's brows went up. "I'd be dead," he said. "Why isn't he?"

"The tree saved him," Wren said, grinning at Hawk's astonishment.

He sent one more look at Connor, a long, considering one, then went forward again without further comment.

They walked in silence until noon. By then the snow was falling thickly. Wren did not hear who suggested a stop. She

172

was just glad when those ahead halted in the lee of a heavy fir tree. Too tired to try scrying, Wren hunched into her cloak and watched the vague figures move back and forth. Suddenly a fire crackled merrily, and snow melted into a pot set on a stone near it.

She heard Tyron's quiet voice: "I've some tea."

And one of Hawk's people: "Save it for tonight. We've chocolate here."

The normalcy of their voices—the way they all seemed to be getting along—made Wren feel peculiar, as if in a dream.

When it was her turn for the hot chocolate, Wren at first just held the cup without drinking, enjoying the warmth. She sank down wearily onto a boulder. A step nearby made her look up.

Brushing aside a branch, Hawk sat down next to her. "At this rate it'll take three days," Hawk said. "I suggest you talk Connor into going with Marla and Alif to my camp. You and the wizard can move faster."

"What then?" Wren asked.

"You get into that camp, let 'em know what's about to happen," Hawk said with a shrug. "If they have any brains they'll fall back—fast."

"But . . ." Wren shook her head. Hawk did not care if Fortian Rhismordith wouldn't listen to a magic prentice and a journeymage. She had finally understood why Hawk was warning them. This was his way of paying back what he considered his debt to Wren, for saving his people from Andreus. Which meant he did have *some* kind of a code of honor— which should include telling the truth, at least about this situation.

So she said, "How do you know all this about the attack?"

"There are places where things usually happen," Hawk said. "I've made it my business to put people there to watch and to report."

He's got a spy system, Wren thought. *And a thorough one, too, from the looks of that map that Andreus burned.*

"What else can you tell me?" Wren asked.

Apparently Hawk was quite willing to talk. *Showing off,* Wren thought.

"Fortian lost both his battles with the Lirwanis. His gang of toffs broke and ran—had to, after those losses. He has no idea how to place his mounted or foot soldiers—thinks the noble way is to line 'em up and charge. And he won't listen to Thule or Rollan or anyone else with experience."

"Prince Rollan is with him?"

"Was." Hawk grinned. "You didn't know that? Left in disgust. Now he's in the east with a gang of tough Siradi border riders, and they've given Andreus a bad time. Too bad your Duke won't listen to him. Together they could give the Lirwanis a serious run for a few years."

"A few *years?*"

Hawk shrugged. "Sure. Their forces are too small to do much more, even if Rhismordith could hold them all together. But Andreus has the big numbers, and the will. And the time." He got to his feet. "Drink up. Talk to Connor. We move out shortly."

Wren sipped at the chocolate. It was grainy and slightly bitter, so different from the creamy, sweet chocolate Queen Astren used to serve.

She's gone now, and even if we win, there will never again be chocolate parties, with Queen Astren singing old folk songs. As grief squeezed her heart, Hawk's words came back to her: *They'd give Andreus a serious run for a few years. A few years!*

Wren thought about the destruction she'd already seen. No matter who won, it would take years to rebuild Cantirmoor. And nothing could make the shattered families whole again.

Finishing her chocolate in one gulp, she cleaned her cup, thinking hard. *There's got to be a way to end this soon!*

She marched out to Tyron and Connor, who looked up expectantly.

"Hawk says we have to be fast, and he thinks you ought to

go to their camp, Connor. You can't run anymore—you ought to be in bed a month!"

"I'd like to sleep for a year," he said. "But what about Teressa?"

"You can leave her to me," Wren said. "Hawk told me plenty."

To her surprise, Connor slowly nodded. "Very well," he said.

And soon he was out of sight, walking slowly up a different trail with two of Hawk's people. Tyron and Wren set out with the rest, Hawk going at a much faster pace than before. Wren was soon overheated in her gritty clothes, but she toiled grimly after, hoping they'd be in time.

They marched single file through a brief, fierce snowstorm, each holding on to the shoulder of the person ahead, and did not stop until it was completely dark. Before they circled up in a cramped little space to camp, Hawk pointed out the glimmer of fires on the slope below.

"That's their camp," he said. "We can reach it by midmorning."

"What about Andreus?" Tyron asked.

Hawk shrugged. "We'll know when he hits them. No way to find out beforehand where he is."

But I can warn them, Wren thought, pulling out her scrystone.

Once again, she could not reach Laris. So she curled up in her cloak.

Yet sleep was impossible. Sitting up, Wren slid her hand into her pack. A short distance away a silhouette also sat up.

"What are you doing?" Hawk demanded.

"Going to find Teressa," Wren said.

Before he could move, she took out the necklace and cast it over her head. Her vision rippled and changed. In the familiar owl form, she gripped her bag, spread her wings, and took off.

With the owl's superb night vision she looked back, saw

175

others sitting up in confusion with Hawk standing in their center, envy clear in his face.

She flew straight up into the dark sky, circling about until she had seen not only Teressa's camp but, just beyond the forest, the terrifying sight of Andreus's army, neatly ordered tents in uncountable rows.

Journeying back, she spiraled down to Teressa's camp, landing among the trees just beyond the tents in order to change. First she shifted to a human so she could hang her knapsack on a tree branch. The dizziness was momentary. Then she changed again, this time into a small white cat. The vertigo lasted longer. As soon as she had her cat vision, she loped soundlessly toward Teressa's tent, ignoring how thoroughly nasty the wet, cold snow felt on her paws.

The sentries never noticed her; not far away she heard the soft whine of a dog.

Slinking around to the back of the tent, she slipped inside.

Seeing that Teressa was alone, she shrugged the necklace off. This time vertigo smote her hard, forcing her to lie down until the dizziness passed. *I don't think I can do this again. Not without a rest.*

As soon as she could sit up, she touched Teressa's shoulder. "Tess," she whispered. "It's Wren."

Teressa stiffened under Wren's hand, then bent to the other side of her cot. A moment later Wren felt a warm, heavy cloak pulled over her head.

"I hope this muffles our voices," Teressa whispered softly. "Who'll hear?"

"Fortian brought one of Carla's maids." Teressa sounded sour. "She spies on me all day. Though I refuse to let her sleep here, she's in the next tent. Now, what's going on?"

"Get ready," Wren warned. "This is going to be a long one."

As Wren talked, she could not see Teressa's reaction, but she heard it. Teressa sat bolt upright, her breathing fast. When Wren stopped at last, Teressa flung off the cloak. "Defeated—

twice? That's not what I was told! I've been asleep," she said. "Oh, not like this, but asleep *here*." Teressa slapped her forehead. "And to think of the days I've spent feeling like a failure, and enduring his little reminders of how a queen ought to think, and behave, until I've begun to believe he really does know best. Give me a light."

Wren snapped a witch-light, and in its cool blue glow stared in surprise at her friend. Teressa had changed in the few weeks the girls had been apart. She was thin, even sharp faced. With her short hair swinging about her shoulders, she looked incongruously like Garian. Her large gray-blue eyes were her father's, though, and they glittered angrily.

"You say Idres has been protecting me?" Her face disappeared briefly as she pulled on some clothes and straightened them quickly. "By magic?"

"That's what Hawk said. Andreus couldn't trace you. Idres's wards are too strong even for him. Then the Duke's army led him straight here."

"I wonder why she did it," Teressa murmured, handing Wren a battered book. "Put this in your bag, will you? It's got all my decisions, the things I've learned. I don't want Carlas's spy to find it, and I don't have time to hide it now."

Wren tucked the book into her tunic as Teressa flung the tent flaps open. In a clear voice she said to the guards, "Stand aside!"

Teressa marched between them, straight to the big blue tent. "Uncle Fortian," she announced, "Andreus is about to attack."

For a moment there was no sound whatever, then Wren heard voices all around, and a dog barking excitedly. Someone lit a torch, then another. In their ruddy light, people appeared. The Duke stepped from the blue tent, his tunic rumpled from being slept in, his hair messy. Squinting against the torchlight, his mouth thin with anger, he snapped, "What?"

"Andreus is on his way."

"Did you discover this in your dreams?" he asked acidly.

Several people laughed.

Teressa flushed. She gestured to Wren. "Tell them what you saw."

Fortian waited until Wren was done talking, then turned to Teressa. "Young as you are, you cannot be too young to understand that the responsible ruler does not turn out an entire army on the word of a child."

"I'm sorry I'm young, and that I made mistakes," Teressa said, her voice high. "I'm sorry I didn't face you when my parents were killed, and that I ran away afterward. But I am sorriest about *your* mistakes, for you are hurting more people than I have—"

"Dear child," Fortian interrupted. "A public brangle is needless."

"I'm sorry," Teressa said, louder, "that you wouldn't listen to Mistress Thule or my uncle Rollan, who *do* know something about battles—"

"Teressa," Fortian cut in. "Permit me to remind you that even princesses owe their relatives the courtesy of good manners—"

Teressa clasped her hands. "Do not," she commanded, "interrupt me again. I am my father's heir—I am now the Queen—and I will be heard!"

Somewhere in the crowd, several people cheered. It was a subdued cheer, but Wren was sure she recognized Garian Rhismordith's voice among them.

Teressa said, "I just wish I'd had the courage to face you before. It's true that you've years and experiences that I don't have, but my father taught me enough about ruling to be certain that your kind of government is not what this country needs. You want to rule, but for whom? Not for the people, not for the land. The roads in your province are rotten, the village walls fall apart so that roaming outlaws attack easily. Yet you've plenty of tax money to build up a private army, and to add another wing to your palace!"

This time the cheer was louder.

"I know I'm too young," Teressa went on. "I know I am not yet ready to rule. But if I'm to have a regent, I want to have someone who has the good of the country at heart, not just power and glory—"

A horn interrupted, wildly blown. The sound echoed through the forest.

"Attack!" came a voice from the darkness. "The Lirwanis are coming!"

Chapter Twenty-Five

*T*eressa's mind went completely blank. She had been concentrating so hard on her confrontation with her uncle that she had forgotten Andreus.

Now the entire camp was looking to her—not to her uncle, but to *her,* for orders.

And she couldn't think of anything to say.

A bubble of hysterical laughter welled inside her. *Why is it in the plays the new ruler knows exactly what to do to get everyone organized for the next crisis?*

But as she scanned the waiting faces, her eye was caught by Garian. He nodded toward Rett, mouthing the word, "Defense."

"Defense," Teressa repeated. Then, louder, "Defense plan!" She pointed at her group leaders, and just like in all the endless drills they ran in orderly groups to get their weapons and take their positions. Watching them, Teressa felt a little of the old thrill. They would be few to Andreus's many. *But at least we will give them a good fight,* she thought.

Then the Lirwanis rode into the camp at full gallop, and the quiet forest was assailed with light—fire and magical—and with the noise of weapons and shouts.

Teressa turned around, trying desperately to make sense of the battle. A terrifying confusion smote her instead, mixing together the smells of burning and fear-sweat, the screams of those who had taken wounds, the flash of red-edged swords, and falling figures in the glaring firelight.

"What should I do?" she asked Wren, hardly aware that she'd spoken.

Wren gripped her hand. Before she could speak, a group of mounted Lirwani soldiers burst through a line of defenders, trampling those who were in their way.

Their leader looked around, then pointed his sword straight at Teressa.

"To me!" Duke Fortian roared. And, as some of his guard rallied, he ran forward, yelling, "Defend the Queen!"

Teressa watched the horrible scene unfold before her with the slowness of a nightmare. The Lirwani leader raised a black glove, and blue witch-light flared out from his fingers like lightning, hovering overhead in a glowing haze. In that pitiless light Teressa saw everything: the faceless Lirwanis in their steel helms riding toward her. The defenders rushing desperately to form a line. The Duke with his sword in his right hand, bending to snatch up a fallen man's sword with his left. The one look he sent Teressa before he turned to face the attackers.

And then Fortian Rhismordith ran right at the two riders in the front of the charging line, both blades whirling.

"Uncle Fortian—" Teressa shouted.

Mud and snow churned up, covering horses and riders. Teressa stumbled forward, eyes on the confusing tangle of bodies. Suddenly the space before her was clear as two horses dashed away, riderless, and two Lirwani soldiers fell dead on either side of the still figure whose lifeless hands each clutched a sword. All around him Lirwanis and Meldrithi fought desperately, but Teressa scarcely heeded them.

"Father!" Garian screamed, from somewhere behind.

"Uncle Fortian," Teressa said numbly, stepping toward him.

"Come." Wren grabbed Teressa's arm. "There's nothing you can do."

Teressa did not resist as Wren tugged her away. Behind them the fighting still raged, but Teressa was only distantly aware of it. Instead, memory made her see, over and over, the way her uncle had fallen defending her.

"Tess!" Wren peered into her face. "Listen. Andreus is looking for you, so I'm going to cast an illusion over you. You won't be able to see very well. Do you hear me?"

Numb with shock, Teressa heard herself answer, "I hear you."

Wren muttered softly next to her, and then the lights smeared, as if seen through tears. But Teressa's eyes were dry—dry and burning.

"All right," Wren said. "That's done. Now let's go." Wren's small, capable hand closed tightly onto Teressa's wrist. "Walk."

Obediently Teressa walked, buffeted by distorted sound. Shutting her eyes against the blurring lights, she moved forward until a flash of pain across her eyelids made her jump.

"*Yow!*" Wren exclaimed, dropping her hand. "What—uh-oh."

Teressa looked up, her vision clear again. All around them desperate battles raged, but right through the thick of it rode a solitary figure on horseback, his cloak thrown carelessly over one shoulder.

In the reddish glow of burning trees Teressa recognized Andreus. He scanned the battlefield, then lifted his head to face her. Though they were still some distance apart, she could see his smile.

Wren muttered softly, and Teressa blinked as illusory trees flickered into existence between her and the Lirwanis. But a moment later they winkled away, destroyed by a casual gesture from Andreus.

Wren gasped a warning before a weird greenish fire lanced directly at them—flared, then vanished. Heat tingled in Teressa's fingers and toes.

"His spell didn't work," Wren said. "That's got to be Idres helping—"

Andreus frowned, still ignoring the battle raging around him. Lifting his hands, he spoke, and this time an ugly light glowed around his fingers.

"Run!" Laris dashed toward them. "Wren, get her away!" Laris whirled around, bringing up her scry-stone. "I'll make a ward-spell—"

"Laris, don't!" Wren cried, but the journeymage was concentrating so fiercely she didn't seem to hear.

A glowing spear of light beamed from Laris's stone toward the Sorcerer-King. He gestured sharply, then pointed. Laris's light dissipated like fog, lanced through by Andreus's red light, a blood-colored glow that now surrounded Laris with nightmarish clarity.

"Laris!" Wren cried, holding out her hands.

But Laris crumpled slowly to the ground, her black hair fanning out against the white snow.

A horn suddenly blared and a charge from behind made the chaos shift direction. For a moment Andreus was hidden from view, then a hard hand gripped Teressa's shoulder, making her jump.

She jerked around, to look up into Hawk's firelit face.

"Run," he said.

"I can't," she said numbly. "Have to stay and see it through."

Hawk shook his head. "Andreus is after *you*. Disappear, and so will the Lirwanis."

"Who are those reinforcements?" Wren asked, pointing behind them.

Tyron appeared at Teressa's other side. "Wood mites, transformed. Unfortunately it won't take long for Andreus to figure that out."

"So *run*." Hawk gave Teressa a push. "We'll sidetrack him a bit."

Teressa felt Wren's hand slide into hers, warm through both pairs of mittens. Teressa was shocked to see the sheen of tears on Wren's face. *I've never seen her cry,* she thought. *Not once, not even in the orphanage.*

The din of battle faded behind them, but the scent of burning lingered in Teressa's nostrils. Horrible sounds seemed to echo inside her skull. *This is what battle is really about,* she thought. *Not banners waving, or fun drills, or heroic words. It's blood and death and destruction.*

"There's got to be some way to end it," she muttered out loud.

To her surprise, Wren answered: "There is."

"What is it—besides more fighting?"

Wren gave a quick shake of her head. "Have to talk to Connor first."

Connor? I'll see Connor, Teressa thought, and began to walk faster.

For what seemed an endless time she and Wren made their way up a steep mountain path. Wren kept stopping to look back or to check the stone on her finger. Finally it glowed, and she gave a short sigh of relief. "Let's wait—the others are trying to find us," she said.

Teressa leaned against a gritty, cold stone. Presently she heard the thud of feet coming up the trail, and there were Hawk, Tyron, and the rest of Hawk's gang, their soot-streaked faces triumphant in the wavering light of a torch.

"We decoyed 'em," Tyron said proudly. "Though I have a feeling Idres was helping. Any of them who do come this way will walk right into a hefty stone-spell. That was Hawk's doing."

"Something I learned from Andreus himself," Hawk said with a gloating laugh. "But we'd best be on the move." He looked back down the line. "Single file! And stay quiet."

Teressa gritted her teeth as they started out at a brisk pace.

Another snowstorm cloaked them as they labored up the mountainside. Teressa bowed her head before the fierce wind, wishing it would numb her heart. They climbed up and up, long after she ceased feeling her feet in their boots.

Hawk called one stop, when they reached a ledge out of the wind. Teressa sank down onto a stone, rousing when someone thrust a flagon at her and said, "Drink." She swallowed some kind of spiced liquor and gasped. It burned like fire going down, but it woke her up.

Nearby, Wren stamped her feet and swung her arms, her knapsack bobbing on her back. Tyron, who had been standing nearby watching, came forward. "Feel better?"

"I'll make it," she said. "What happened to the rest of our people?"

"Kial and Kira were trying to round up your old army," he said. "Some of the Rhismordith Blues stampeded off with someone wearing your old cloak. It was Garian's idea. They led the Lirwanis away from us."

Teressa winced, thinking of Garian's father and how he had died before she could make her peace with him. *I've always disliked him, and I dreaded having to deal with him when this war ends, but I never wanted him to die.*

"Let's move," Hawk said.

Once again they started up the trail. The next stop, after an unmeasurable time, was in a cavern well concealed by drooping ivy. Tyron and Wren glanced down at the crude pattern of stones laid on the floor.

"A Designation," Tyron exclaimed, looking pleased.

Hawk nodded. "If you two can help me transfer everyone, we can save at least a day's journey." He swept his arm around at the others. "More than two multiple transfers in one day is more than I can manage." And as Tyron and Wren assented, he said, "The pattern is the same as this one, and here's what the camp looks like . . ."

After a short conference, the three magicians started transferring people. Teressa's turn came too soon for her taste—the weird nothingness of the transfer magic made her feel dizzy.

When her vision cleared, she faced the curious stares of Hawk's gang. Standing on their periphery was Connor.

Her heart hammered painfully when she saw him. He

smiled at her, but before he could speak, Wren bounded over to him, saying, "Connor! I've got to talk to you!"

Hawk appeared at Teressa's side. "Welcome," he said, bowing with a mocking air.

Teressa glanced about appraisingly. They appeared to be in some kind of stone house, very old, and probably—from the dust and spiderwebs in the corners—long abandoned. "I hope your plans are better than your housekeeping," she said.

He laughed, indicating a low stone bench near the roaring fire. "Let's discuss those plans."

His group moved to various jobs, from preparing food to polishing weapons. Tyron dropped onto a stool by the fire and started poring over a thin book, while Connor and Wren sat nearby, talking softly.

Teressa thought she heard Lirwani words from another room and was momentarily distracted. Facing Hawk, she said, "First, I want to know what you're getting out of this. I know you didn't rescue me out of cousinly kindness."

Hawk laughed. "I snatched you to score off Andreus. It's a payback to Idres . . . and to my cousin Farle, who saved my life when I was small." Teressa saw Tyron's head lift suddenly, but he said nothing. Hawk smiled a little, then went on. "Payback also to your prentice friend with the stripy hair, who thought fast in a hot moment."

This time Tyron did speak. "Wren? You didn't tell me that!"

Wren looked up, her face crimson. "I guess I forgot," she said.

Everyone laughed, which eased some of the tension.

Teressa said to Hawk, "Look. I don't know if I'll get my throne back, but if I do, what is it that you want?"

"To be left alone."

Teressa bit her lip. There were very few of her people living in Rhiscarlan land anymore. She said, "What about traders who pass down the east road to Hroth Falls?"

"Free to come and go," Hawk said with a shrug. "They don't bother us, we don't bother them."

"And three years from now? Five? Supposing your friends here decide a raid into Meldrith might be fun?"

"Then beat them back," Hawk said. "If you're asking if I have designs on your throne, no. If you want a promise of eternal loyalty, I won't give you that, either." He finished with a challenging look.

Time to practice compromise, then. Though he's not likely to be a friend, at least I can work to keep him from becoming an enemy.

"From my studies of history, such promises usually aren't worth the paper they're written on," Teressa said, and saw a glint of approval in Hawk's black eyes. "Right now I want to end this war, as fast as I can. But how?"

"You win by brute force or by cleverness," he said.

"Force," Teressa repeated, wincing. "We can't win that way, not this year, not in ten. How can Andreus make the Lirwanis fight that long? Can we suborn them somehow? Or do they live for fighting?"

"No," came a voice from the corner. A thin girl with reddish blond hair put down her stitchery and said in a strong Lirwani accent, "Not all. It's just, there is no choice. Each ten years the sector captain comes, to take the strongest boy or girl from every family. Desertion, or cowardice, or any other infraction, means the entire family is punished. So they obey, even if they do not like the orders. They must." She bent her head over her sewing again.

Into the silence came Wren's quiet voice. "I think I know a way."

Everyone in earshot stopped. For a long moment no one spoke.

"What?" Hawk exclaimed at last.

Wren whispered briefly to Connor, who nodded slowly, then she turned to Tyron. "We use that book of Andreus's." She pointed to the Lirwani girl. "We'll ask them to translate the spells written in Lirwani, and if we find the ones that bind the land, we release these spells."

Hawk whistled. "You got *that* book?" He stood up and held out his hand. "Let me see it."

"No," Tyron said.

No one spoke. Hawk took another step toward Tyron, and Teressa wondered how long she, Tyron, Connor, and Wren could last against all of Hawk's gang.

But Hawk did not attack Tyron or give the order for him to be attacked. "Why?" he asked, his eyes narrowed.

Tyron met that look squarely. "Because you knew what book was meant."

A short laugh escaped Hawk, then he turned around abruptly. "Right," he said. "Right. I know its power—but I also know its cost. Keep it away from me, would you?"

Tyron gave him a twisted smile. "It's loaded with magic. Wards, I suspect—against Idres, and Halfrid, and probably you as well."

"And tracers," Hawk said.

Tyron nodded soberly. "I know. Though I did my best to foul those."

Hawk turned to the Lirwani girl. "Nasrya, will you help him with that?"

The girl set aside her mending project and rose to her feet.

Tyron and Nasrya left the room. Hawk turned to Wren. "So you lift the land spells, but then what? There's a good chance the change back will kill every living thing within four days' travel."

Wren turned to Connor. "Not," she said, "if it gets some help."

Hawk's eyes narrowed. "What kind of magic are we talking about?"

Connor said nothing. It was Wren who hesitated, then after a slight nod from Connor, said, "Iyon Daiyin magic. The land spells bind their magic too. If it's released, well, maybe we can prevent what you said."

"A big maybe." Hawk pursed his lips. "But it could stop the war. So what now? Issue an ultimatum—if Andreus doesn't leave by a certain time—say, Rhis Day—we release his land-bindings? What about everyone else? It'll be rough here, but Senna Lirwan is going to be hit really hard. At least as hard as the ancient cataclysms that wrenched the land into its present form."

"We'll have to warn everyone—on both sides, in both countries," Wren said, turning to one of the Lirwanis. "Or do you think this plan isn't fair to your people?"

The boy answered with low-voiced intensity, "For my family to see the sun again, and feel rain, and see things grow? Release your spells. We will go home to warn them, even though it means death if we are caught."

Several conversations broke out then, everyone with an idea to share. Teressa stared at Connor, who was being pelted with questions from two or three people. For the first time ever, he was willing to let outsiders find out about his background. Why? What had happened?

She rose and looked out of one of the little windows. *He's the one who left, so I will wait for him to come to me.* And then, remembering their last conversation, she also remembered her promise, and resolutely began viewing the scene outside the window.

At first it was hard to concentrate. Thoughts kept whirling through her head. But as she studied the bluish icicles, the soft gleam of snow-dusted peaks, the subtle colorations of the frozen stream beside the house, her mind calmed. *It really is beautiful,* she thought. *He was right about beauty being there for the seeing.*

A few moments later, hearing his step, she was about to tell him. But he touched his finger to her lips.

Seen close, it was startling how much his face had changed. She could not define his expression—except it was *different.* "When I was little," he said, "my father told me to keep my talents a secret. He said if I revealed them I'd always

189

be an outcast, even in my own family. He was right—except those things no longer matter, just as political boundaries no longer matter."

"Political boundaries?" Teressa repeated. "Is that a dig at me?"

Connor reached to take her hands. "No," he said. "I'm being stupid and clumsy. It's just that I had an experience that makes me see things differently. I have to find out how to use my talents better. I have to find my own kind of people, even if if means traveling to the other side of the world."

"Even if it takes a lifetime?" she asked, letting go of his hands.

His eyes were steady. "Yes."

"So nonmagical people don't matter anymore?"

"They do matter," he said. "Always. Every living thing matters."

But not me. I don't matter to him. Not the way I want to. I lost my parents before I could learn to rule, I lost my uncle before I could learn to compromise, and now I've lost Connor . . .

But none of that could be said out loud. She summoned up a smile and said, "Well, you'll always be welcome back home. I hope you know that."

"Teressa—" He half lifted a hand.

Though I can't have love, I won't take pity. She tossed her hair back and said with her best court brightness, "Hadn't we better plan how to word our ultimatum to Andreus? Or is that my job?"

He turned away, and a moment later she heard him talking to Wren and Tyron, his voice calm and unemotional.

She looked back out at the frozen stream.

Shall I laugh at myself for counting up all the pretty sights in order to impress him?

She smiled, and she kept smiling even after the colors had blurred and blended and the hot tears, so long denied, washed the last of the battle smoke from her cheeks.

Chapter Twenty-Six

*T*his Day had come at last.

Tyron, Connor, and Teressa sat watching Wren as she slowly pulled out her scry-stone and looked into it.

Wren's heart thumped warningly as she scryed for Andreus.

"Nothing," she said finally, setting her scry-stone down. "No sign of Andreus anywhere." Relief made her knees wobbly.

"He doesn't believe us," Teresa said.

"Maybe." Tyron shook his head.

Teressa rose to her feet. "Well, it is a holiday. Let us celebrate by having supper, and then it will be time to release the spells."

Tyron followed her out, Wren walking more slowly. She passed a window, stopping to look out across the snowy mountain peaks.

She did not know whose house they were in—they had moved so much during the swiftly passing days since the decision to remove the land-bindings that she sometimes lost track of what town they were in.

Fleeting memories ghosted across the quiet landscape. The long lines of refugees moving westward to the hills, the faces in towns, villages, farms when Wren told them about the ultimatum to Andreus.

She had visited the last of the villages on her list that morning and had found it completely deserted.

191

She glanced around the little room. Would this house even be standing by nightfall? She looked at the carving above the fireplace and the hand-painted twining ivy leaves around the windows. They were faded, generations old.

Turning away, she moved into the brightly lit main room, where the others were gathering around a big table, except for the dog Tip, who lay on the floor, tail thumping.

"Wren?" Teressa said. "There you are. Eat up while it's hot!" She paused, her eyes narrowing. "Are you all right?"

Wren plopped down onto a floor pillow. "Are we doing the right thing?"

Teressa and Tyron exchanged a look, and Tyron grinned ruefully. "Want to know what we were just talking about?"

Connor looked up from helping himself to the food. "Did anyone argue with you when you went to warn them?"

"No," Wren said. "And Kira said the same. They just looked at us as if thinking, *Here's another thing to cope with.*"

Teressa nodded. "People's lives have been so torn up, another cataclysm doesn't seem to make much difference. If we'd announced a year ago that we were going to do this, there would have been riots."

Wren got up and moved to the table. There she found mute evidence that the rest of the winter would be hard, whatever happened after they released the land spells: all they had to eat for this holiday meal was oatmeal with thin slices of apple added. Scooping some into a bowl, careful to take no more than her share, she sat down with the others.

"Any news?" Teressa asked, breaking into her thoughts.

"Just a relayed message from Hawk," Wren said. "Some bands of outlaws were spotted riding east toward Arakee. Probably on a looting spree."

"They were warned, weren't they?"

"If Hawk kept his promise," Wren said. "He wouldn't tell us who or where his messengers are, but he promised to spread the word to both sides."

"Then let's enjoy our last Rhis Day meal together," Teressa said, and Wren saw that someone had managed to find green-and-white candles, and had decorated the windowsills and the mantelpiece with green boughs.

Tyron had brewed up the last of his tea, and they all lifted their cups, in silence, then drank.

Wren felt her heart constrict and saw her own emotions in Teressa's bright eyes, in the tense way Tyron sat, in Connor's somber face as he shared his meal with Tip.

Rhis Day is a family holiday, but our families are either out of reach or gone forever.

They talked very little as they ate, and when they were done, Connor collected the bowls and took them out to wash. Tyron said, "Wren? Shall we try one last time?"

Wren went to get her scry-stone, thinking, *What if Andreus does promise to leave? Can we believe him?*

Cradling her scry-stone in her hands, she concentrated on masking herself. Then she listened. She caught swift whispers of messages between unknown magicians and sensed a great many minds waiting—listening. But not Andreus.

She said, "Andreus of Senna Lirwan, it is now Rhis Day." And braced herself, waiting—

Nothing.

Setting down her stone, she looked up at the others. "That's it."

Tyron waited until she had stowed away her scry-stone, then they all hefted their knapsacks and walked outside the house, onto the hillside. Fresh snow dusted everything, looking clean and bright in the late-afternoon light. No one was around, not even a bird. When Wren and Kira had gone on their mission to warn people, Connor had communicated word of the impending danger to birds and beasts.

"Ready?" Tyron asked, and when they assented, he moved a little away from them all and carefully set his bag down. He said, "We'll meet at the Magic School Destination, right?"

Seating herself on a low stone, Wren nodded quickly, not

193

trusting herself to speak. There were a lot of *ifs* between now and then.

She glanced up at Connor, saw him watching the mountain peaks behind her as one hand ruffled absently at Tip's ears. He seemed to become aware of her staring, and he smiled reassuringly. Of all of them, he probably had the most dangerous job, yet he seemed the least worried.

Tyron took the slim book from his pack and laid it carefully on a rock. Then he stepped backward and wiped his hands down his sides. Wren saw a tremble in his fingers, which despite the icy air were bare. Then he stepped to the edge of a high cliff and started his magic.

He's practiced it—lots, Wren realized, listening to the swift, sure singsong of his voice. The air seemed still and glittery now, charged with magic potential as one by one he reversed the Lirwani binding-spells.

After the second or third, Wren sensed changes in the air around her, though she heard and saw nothing out of the ordinary. The world around her seemed to be waiting, poised.

Tyron's voice flattened, but he spoke steadily until he reached the last spell. By now the air felt heavy and fever warm. Wren squinted at Tyron, whose outline wavered as if seen through water. The power he'd summoned intensified, making her skin prickle. Tyron raised his glowing hands, brought them slowly together, his muscles straining as if against a terrible weight. Greenish lightning flickered—in horror Wren realized it came from the book on the rock. Then Tyron ended the spell, and Wren's vision swam dizzily at the vast sense of release.

She shook her head violently. "The book," she croaked. "Lightning—"

That was all the warning they had.

Instinct plunged Wren's hand into her own knapsack just as Andreus appeared, dressed for battle, with both knife and sword at his side.

"Here you are," he said as Tyron grabbed up the book and stood on the very edge of the cliff, his face, pale from the effort

194

he'd just expended, determined. "I'll take that book," Andreus said.

Deep in the mountain beneath them stones rumbled as if in warning, and the ground shook slightly. Teressa staggered, looking terrified. Connor met Wren's gaze, motioning downward.

She knew what he was thinking: *If Connor doesn't reach that Iyon Daiyin magic and soon, there's going to be mountain-sized trouble.*

Except they had sorcerer-sized trouble right in front of them.

"No," Tyron said, holding the book high. "I'm going to destroy it if I can."

"You can't," Andreus said, smiling. "You don't know enough magic. This"—he lifted a hand, indicating the mountains around them—"is just a small part of the knowledge it contains. You controlled that land spell well enough. I could teach you much more powerful spells. You could take this kingdom, or one larger."

"Even if I believed you," Tyron said, stepping forward, "I'd still—"

But Andreus was not interested in Tyron. Now that his book was not in danger, he waved a quick, complicated sign. Too drained to fight the magic, Tyron flung the book into Wren's lap, then collapsed into the snow.

Wren closed one hand on the book, keeping the other in her bag. A moment later she felt Connor at one side, and Teressa moved to join her on the other side. *Ward-spells, ward-spells,* Wren thought desperately.

A loud rumble beneath them was followed by another strong tremor. Tip flattened his ears and growled at Andreus.

Andreus ignored both tremor and dog. Studying Wren, he said, "Who are you?"

"Wren."

"Ah." The sorcerer looked interested, his manner that of someone who has all day to chat. Another tremor shook the ground, sending stones and snow tumbling off the edge of the cliff very near where Tyron lay. Wren swallowed, trying to still her thundering heart.

Andreus said, "I'm told you are the one who pinched the Princess—and these others as well—from my castle three years ago." His eyes narrowed. "And—didn't I see you among Hawk Rhiscarlan's rabble recently?"

"I'm not one of his followers," Wren said. On the edge of her vision she saw Tyron move weakly, and hope flared inside her. *Keep Andreus talking!* "But I did upend you with a nice shift-spell. Great fun it was, too."

Andreus seemed to enjoy her gloat. "A spawn of the Iyon Daiyin, are you? Very far from your people, and lately in the guise of a student. Why?"

He thinks I'm a real magician! Which means . . .

A harder tremor made them all stagger. In the distance a mighty crack echoed, sending a cloud of dust and dirt mushrooming into the air. Wren shook her head, trying to clear it of distracting thoughts. *Which means he thinks I'm a strong enough magician to destroy his book.* "I'm learning things," she said, and saw impatience tighten Andreus's mouth. She knew she could not fight him in a magic battle—which he would begin the moment he stopped finding her interesting. "Speaking of your castle, you'll find a surprise waiting," she said quickly.

Andreus's brows lifted. "Should I thank you for the warning? What is it, a creative trap set by Idres Rhiscarlan—or is it the lady herself?"

"Something you'd never dream of," Wren said, thinking of the pie-bed and the knotted clothes. *Oh Idres, where are you now?*

Probably watching—or maybe not. But she had given Wren a gift. Remembering the necklace, Wren wormed her fingers deeper into her bag, trying to keep Andreus from noticing her movement.

A low rumble grew beneath them, gaining strength as the

196

ground shook. Connor fought for balance nearby. Teressa clung to a gnarled tree. Wren turned away, closing her fingers on the hard stone of the necklace. A plan materialized in her head.

"We can discuss this in more comfort elsewhere," Andreus said. His voice was still even, but Wren saw a vein beating in his temple. "Give me my book, and I'll include you in the transfer. Otherwise, I'll leave you to enjoy the results of what you've done here."

As he spoke, a crack appeared in the very edge of the cliff, just behind him, and with a loud roar, that portion of the cliff disappeared from sight.

Andreus looked behind quickly, then stepped toward Wren, one hand out, the other pulling the knife. "Give it to me. *Now.*"

"Try to take it, you fungus-faced muffin," Wren screamed, and yanked the necklace over her head.

Andreus sent a terrible spell at her, but the magic failed before the greater magic of the necklace, causing only a moment of red heat. The familiar vertigo warred with the shaking ground, but Wren held control as she transformed into a mighty falcon.

Shrieking *Kek-kek-kek,* Wren took flight directly over Andreus's head. She reached with her claws, and he ducked aside, slashing at her with the knife. The ground shook hard, causing him to stumble, and she saw her moment. Pulling in her head, she snagged the necklace with a claw. Then she fell toward Andreus, flinging the necklace over his head and envisioning him as a mouse.

She landed hard and almost blacked out. When her vision cleared, she saw Teressa holding a small, struggling gray shape, the necklace wound so tightly about its neck it could not get the magic thing off. "Let's get out of here," Teressa yelled.

But transfer magic buffeted them—and Idres appeared, her dark gown and long black hair waving in the rising wind.

"Well done, Wren," she said. "Give me that book, and then we'd all better leave."

"It's evil," Wren said, holding it away. "We have to destroy it."

Idres shook her head. "It's just a book that has been put to evil purpose. I won't do that. Quickly, child! Don't you see the danger we are all in?"

She knows I'm just a prentice, Wren thought. Then she met Connor's eyes, remembering everything he had said about Iyon Daiyin magic. *Iyon Daiyin? Me?*

There would never be a better time to try.

Wren could sense magic potential around them, even stronger than before—despite the shaking mountains, the air seemed to scintillate with magic. She took the book in both hands, fixed an image of fire in her mind, and a sudden blast of golden light made her blink away.

Heat singed her hands, and she dropped the book onto the snow. It fell open, and for a moment the dark brown words glowed bright yellow, then there was another flash, and all that was left of Andreus's book was a pile of gray ash.

Idres grabbed the necklace-bound mouse from Teressa and vanished.

Tyron got slowly to his feet. "Is it too late?"

"I have to try," Connor said. "But take Tip."

"I'll stay and help," Wren said, still dazed from what she had done. Shaking herself, she said more firmly to Tyron, "You two go."

Tyron took Teressa's hand, touched the dog's head, and transferred.

Wren turned to Connor. "I'm afraid about this cliff—"

"Let's get away from here," Connor answered. "Can you use the tree where you found me as a Designation?"

Wren hesitated. She knew powerful magicians could transfer to places besides Destinations, but she had never dared. She shut her eyes, recalling vividly that tree with its gnarled limbs. She could see it as clearly as any Designation tile pattern.

"Easy," Wren said, opening her eyes. "I'll never forget that place."

She reached. His fingers closed around hers, warm and strong and reassuring. She shut her eyes and once again—carefully—pictured that tall, spreading tree. Then she said the transfer spell.

Gray nothingness closed in on her, cold and strange. When it cleared, they stood before the tree. Snowdrifts completely covered the place where Connor had been lying.

He dropped down next to the tree. Wren scrabbled through her bag, pulling out her scry-stone. Then she looked over at Connor, who sat very still, his breath making little puffs of white. Another tremor rumbled beneath them.

She rearranged herself more comfortably, trying to shut out the coldness of the snow in her toes and the wind on her cheeks. Looking down into her scry-stone, she concentrated on Connor, seeing him as a presence near her, warm and bright and steady as a new flame.

He moved toward another presence, one harder to see, so she turned her focus to that. Large and green and slow moving, this presence rejoiced in sun time . . .

It's the tree. I see the tree!

Connor's thought came, clear as if he spoke: *Listen.*

Below the tree lay a vast pool of moon-bright lights, some of them darting about in agitation.

Wren sensed unmeasurable distances. She tried to follow Connor's flame as it glided rapidly into the sea of lights.

As she sank deeper, a rustle of whispering voices reached her. The wordless mutter altered slowly as Connor moved among the lights, causing them to change from an urgent dissonance to a soothing harmony.

Time passed. Wren was no longer aware of her body. She drifted in the mighty sea of voices, dreaming of crumbling mountains; of a spectacular fountain shooting skyward, golden in the fading sunlight; of great rivers splashing in waves over broken land, then smoothing once again into long ribbons of water; of the blue sky filled with swarms of birds;

199

and of fields of snow covered with running, hopping, bounding creatures.

After a very long time the song diminished. One by one the lights moved away, until at last they left the silence of a perfect peace.

Wren found her way back to herself then, and looked up from her scry-stone. She was surprised at how stiff her neck felt.

Cold trickled into her collar as she stretched. Looking down, she discovered a layer of snow blanketing her body. She got to her feet slowly, swinging her arms and stamping.

Connor stood nearby, brushing the snow off his clothes. Wren blinked at him, then made another discovery. "It's morning!" she exclaimed. "How long were we at it?" She made a face. "And what were we at? Did you follow it any better than I did?"

Connor looked around slowly, as though listening for something. Wren looked about as well. The mountain they stood on seemed the same, except for bare contours where the snow had fallen away in giant landslides. To the south, the horizon looked much as it ever had, but to the north—the old border between Meldrith and Senna Lirwan—where there used to be high white peaks, Wren saw stone-studded hills, and beyond those a plain partly covered by water glistening in the sunlight.

"The worst is over," Connor said. "That much I know. Though we were almost too late." He brushed the last of the snow off his sleeve, then smiled. "I don't know about you, but I could stand some breakfast. Think they'll have any at the Magic School?"

Wren laughed.

Chapter Twenty-Seven

They appeared safely at the Magic School Destination. As he'd promised, Tyron was waiting. When he saw them, his face went white with relief. "You're back! You're safe!"

"How is it here?" Wren asked.

"Come on. You'll see," Tyron said. "Teressa camped with some of the others outside the city gates."

"Others?"

"Our people and a few of those who'd hidden in caves below Queen Rose's Garden. Falstan is in the city. So's Duchess Carlas," he added in a dry voice.

"Hoo," Wren said, hefting her knapsack. "I just hope there's some food around. Hey! The School still seems to be standing."

"It's all right—our wards held. Some of the city wasn't so lucky," Tyron said as they walked swiftly from the building. "The quakes were really bad at first, then they settled down into gentle shakes, but they went on all night. Just stopped a little while ago." He looked over, his brown eyes alight with interest. "I suspect somehow that you can tell me about that."

"Later," Connor murmured as they neared the city gate, which still stood, though not much of the wall was connected to it anymore. Before the gate a crowd of people milled, all talking at once. Wren saw Garian, still in his shabby velvet, and Helmburi the steward. Kira and Rett and Kial were all there, looking thin and worn but happy.

Tip bounded forward, ears flying, and behind him Teressa ran, hands outstretched.

"Wren! Connor! You were so long—we thought—" Teressa cried, hugging Wren and glancing over her shoulder at Connor.

Around them other voices rose, demanding, exclaiming, excited.

Wren shook her head, and turned to Connor. "What's going on here? Did you see Idres?"

"No," said a new voice.

The talk died away quickly into whispers as Idres Rhiscarlan walked up to them, cool and remote as always.

"Idres!" Wren exclaimed. "Where's Andreus? Is he still a mouse?"

"Gone," Idres said. "I gave in to the temptation to gloat a little, and gave him his own shape back. He escaped my temporary prison. Not that it matters. You destroyed most of his magic when you torched the Book of Bones, and his soldiery is busily scattering across the blasted landscape homeward. The game is no longer worth playing."

"Game?" Wren repeated blankly.

"*Game!*" Teressa said angrily. "A war—people's lives— and that's a *game?*"

Idres smiled, but her dark eyes were cold. "It was a game for your father when he sneaked into Senna Lirwan nearly twenty years ago, to lure me out. Andreus merely continued the game, until you outfoxed him by ruining the winnings."

"Outfoxed?" Teressa said. "Did you think *we* were playing a game?"

"Weren't you?" the woman said, looking at Tyron, Connor, and Wren. "Testing your powers? And you," she turned to Teressa. "Can you deny that you too have played, however briefly, at the game of kings?"

"You mean war," the Princess said, her eyes huge, her face white.

Wren stepped close to her best friend, but for once Teressa did not even notice her.

202

Idres gestured toward the city. "Still, your motives were better than most, and I am glad you survived. But now you face the task of rebuilding. I remind you that for twelve years you were not taught to think like kings think. Use *that* training now." She looked about her. "You'll need it. We both will."

"What do you mean?" Wren asked.

Idres turned to her. "I mean that Senna Lirwan also must be rebuilt."

Wren gasped. "You're taking over there?"

"Yes. That was *my* training, and I've waited ever since."

"What about Andreus?" Tyron asked soberly.

"When he returns—and he will, if he thinks there's something to be had—I'll be ready," Idres promised. Then she pointed inside the city. "You had better get inside and board up what you can. Your quakes are going to bring on some spectacular weather soon." She walked away, and though Wren called after her again, she simply shook her head—and then vanished.

Teressa sighed. "Let's go see what's left."

The people around them pressed close, pelting them with questions as they picked their way along the rubble-strewn streets. In the strong light of day they looked at cracked walls, houses with roofs fallen in, and here and there burned-out husks or piles of rubble.

A grim mood settled on them all as they made their way to the palace at the center of the city. In the courtyard, they found another group of people waiting—Wren recognized the foremost one, Duchess Carlas Rhismordith. Despite her muddy skirts and unkempt hair, the Duchess marched forward, her head held regally.

"There you are, Teressa," she said crossly. "I overlook the vast discourtesy you have done to your relations by not communicating with us . . ."

Wren dropped back so the woman's sharp voice wouldn't hurt her ears. Finding Tyron nearby, she said, "Do you think we might be able to banish Andreus's wards and contact Master Halfrid and our other magicians?"

Tyron nodded. "That's the first thing I plan to do." He

lifted his head, cocking it slightly. "Second, maybe," he muttered. "First, we eat."

After one polite request to the Duchess to come along if she liked, Teressa did not say anything during the long walk. As they entered the palace, most of the people fell silent. Tyron murmured a spell and the glow-globes ignited, revealing the long hall, a crack up one wall and most of the windows gone.

Rubble dusted the furniture—that which hadn't burned in the fire the night of the Lirwanis' attack.

Teressa still said nothing, just walked across the hall where her father had held court, and continued into the narrower hallway in the back. The Duchess and her entourage followed, the Duchess still talking.

"Is Tess all right?" Wren whispered, thinking of the King's and Queen's deaths.

Connor looked troubled and said nothing.

But Tyron smiled a little grimly. "I know that look. Watch."

Teressa led them down the hall, which was a plain one usually used by servants. The Duchess had noticed and was complaining about that as well.

They reached another room, one relatively free of burns and damage. The room was full of housekeeping supplies.

". . . and we have not had anything hot to drink since yesterday," the Duchess was saying. "Teressa, are you listening? You will need proper guidance, which I am prepared to give you, but first I require a hot meal, on a *clean* plate, and—"

Teressa rummaged on a shelf, then turned around. She held something out to her aunt, who took it, then stared. "What is *this?*" Carlas demanded, her long nose lifting.

"An apron," Teressa said, tying another around her waist. Then she put her hands on her hips and looked around at all the people crowding into the room. "Idres was right—I did spend twelve years learning how to cook, and sew, and clean, and mend. Isn't that lucky?"

Tyron laughed—and one by one, the others all joined in, all except Carlas, who stared at the apron as if it were about to grow fangs and bite her.

Teressa clapped her hands briskly, then reached for a broom. "Shall we get started?"

Epilogue

*W*ren stretched out on the stone wall and turned her face up to the sun. The warm spring breeze ruffled her hair.

After half a year of what seemed to have been unceasing labor, it was good to just sit and be lazy.

She swung her sandaled feet over the edge of the city wall and looked out over the grassy plain. Though the winter had been hard, spring had come at last. So far the spring rains had been gentle, exactly what was needed for growing crops.

"There you are."

She turned—and saw Tyron climbing up the ladder. "Has Orin decided to stay at the Magic School?" she asked.

Tyron nodded. "Falstan gave her the official tour, and when I left to go to the palace she was trying to decide between two girls who each offered to be her roommate." He looked around and stretched. "Teressa said I might find you here."

"Does she need me?" Wren asked, trying not to sound hopeful.

Tyron gave her a considering look as he settled himself onto the wide stone next to her. "She said we ought to give Connor a decent send-off."

Wren turned around and watched the empty road again. She had not talked to anyone about it, but she couldn't help feeling hurt that she saw Teressa so seldom anymore. Of course they had all been busy—it was inevitable that the new Queen would be busiest with all her new duties.

But still Wren felt strange, as if a hole had appeared in her life. *I guess it makes sense. That war changed the land, it changed everyone else's life, so it had to change the four of us as well.*

"This is where I used to sit when Tess was sent on her missions by her father," Wren said. "She'd always turn around when she got to that hill, and wave, and I'd wave back. I thought Connor deserved the same thing—if he thinks to look back."

"You don't think he will?" Tyron asked, grinning.

"What do you mean by that?" Wren demanded.

Tyron shrugged his bony shoulders. "I mean that it was nice for him to wait until you'd passed your journeymage test before he set off on his quest, so it would be nice if you don't send him off alone."

"If it mattered that much, he wouldn't be going off in the first place," Wren muttered. "I mean, you'd think he could at least wait until I finish my project in the caves—if they're still there."

"They will be, I think," Tyron said. "And you can tell Connor about it when you see him next."

Wren snorted. "When we're old and gray. You heard him last night—he said it'll take at least a year just to poke his way south through our continent. Then he crosses the Great Sea. Then—"

"Then in three years, he reaches the Summer Islands, where the direct descendants of the Iyon Daiyin are supposed to live," Tyron said. "I remember. So?"

"So then it takes a dozen years for him to make his way back again!"

Tyron just laughed at her indignation.

Wren tried not to be angry. "Too much has changed," she mumbled.

Tyron's laughter faded, and he nodded. "That's true enough. A lot of the changes are for the good, though, don't you think?"

207

Wren sighed, thinking of the altered landscape, of the new city. Teressa had chosen an artist who knew something of building to redesign what had been destroyed. When the work was finished, Cantirmoor would no longer be a jumble of mismatched houses and roofs, but would be pleasing to the eye no matter where one stood.

She thought of Garian Rhismordith busy learning farming, his fancy palace overrun with refugees all winter. All his father's hoarded tax money had gone to buying food just to see them through the winter, which had left Garian not much better off than any of the people on his family's land. Even his sister, Mirlee, who had always been a pest, had turned her attentions to learning new skills—in her case, negotiating trade deals with outland merchants. She drove a tough bargain.

Some people had adjusted well to the new ways; others had not. The Duchess clung to the old ways, insisting on wearing court gowns and being served on silver. Teressa had done nothing to change this. When she visited Duchess Carlas, she dressed up and observed the court etiquette. "The old ways are a comfort to some people," she'd said to Wren. "And some of the old ways ought to be preserved. I don't mind her—she doesn't give me any trouble anymore."

The only person who gave Teressa trouble, Wren reflected as she covertly eyed Tyron, was the magician sitting right next to her. Halfrid had decided that Tyron's removal of the land-binding spells was as good a master's project as any, and despite his young age, Tyron was now wearing the robes of a master magician. Freed from studying, he was at the palace a lot, and it seemed to Wren that just about every time she saw Tyron and Teressa together, they were arguing about something. Politics, trade, magic, history, even food—anything and everything made their opinions clash. But neither of them seemed to mind a bit.

"There he is," Tyron said.

Below them a figure appeared, tall, broad in the shoulders,

a plump, happy dog trotting at his side. From the back, Connor looked grown up, Wren thought, studying his plain traveling clothes, his old knapsack, the long walking staff.

She bit her lip. *Should I call out to him?* If she'd been alone, she would have.

But then he reached the little hill and stopped, and turned around. In the clear sunlight she could see his grin as he lifted a hand.

She grinned back, waving. Tyron lifted his hand in farewell.

Connor saluted them with his walking stick, then turned around again. He and Tip were soon lost from sight.

Gone. Wren felt an even bigger hole in her life. Too late, she'd realized at his farewell supper—just the four of them, a rare thing anymore—that it had been Connor, not Teressa, who had always listened to her worries about her magic tests, about her plans for her project. It was Connor she'd always had to tell her jokes to first, and Connor who enjoyed her stories. He'd spent a lot of time at the School, helping them move furniture, clean, and get classes organized again. He'd spent time closeted with Halfrid as well, and had been one of the first to welcome Orin when the spring thaws brought her down from her mountain, but mostly he'd just listened to Wren. She hadn't thought to thank him for that, because she'd taken it for granted, all of it. Now he was gone.

She turned around, her feet feeling for the ladder. "I guess I'd better get back to work," she mumbled.

"Right," Tyron agreed promptly. "The sooner you get those cave inscriptions located and copied, the sooner you can get on with your life of adventuring."

"Life of adventuring?" Wren repeated.

"Isn't that what you always used to talk about?" Tyron's brows slanted up under his bird nest of hair.

"I think I've had my fill of adventure," Wren said.

"But it's not always war," Tyron said, now serious. "Have you really changed your mind? I mean, you can—of course—

but there's one person I know who'll be disappointed." He waved his hand at the road.

Wren returned to the wall, looking out at the horizon. She felt the old longings stir again, just a little. Too much had been lost that winter, and too much changed, for her to ever want the same kind of adventures she had dreamed of when she was small, but . . .

She thought of the mysterious outer world—and Idres Rhiscarlan's hints about the kinds of magic she might find there.

Unbidden, she heard Connor's voice from the night before: . . . *three years, the Summer Islands* . . .

Three years. He was telling me where he'll be, so I can find him if I want.

Wren turned her back on the road and started down the ladder again. But this time she was smiling.

5